D0554678

ALSO BY WILLIAM KOTZWINKLE
ELEPHANT BANGS TRAIN

HERMES 3000

William Kotzwinkle

PANTHEON BOOKS

A DIVISION OF RANDOM HOUSE

NEW YORK

ISBN: 0-394-47621-2

Library of Congress Catalog Card Number: 76-175642

Design by Carol Fern Halpert

Manufactured in the United States of America by
The Colonial Press Inc., Clinton, Mass.

FIRST EDITION

AUM MANI PADME HUM
HENRY ANITA MU

. . . AND GREAT MASTER CHING LIANG
EXPLAINED
HOW THE MYRIAD BUDDHA-LANDS
ARE INTERPENETRATING.

FROM THE DREAM OF ZEN MASTER HAN SHAN

chapter 1

"I SEEN HER in that same dress all year."

The Golden Cafeteria was jealously guarded by old women. When one of them departed for the day, pushing through the turnstile and revolving doors, onto Broadway, the others had something to talk about.

"I seen her begging on the corner."

"You're kidding, Gladys."

"I wouldn't kid about such a thing."

The busboys were Puerto Rican. They did not give a damn. The cook was Chinese. He stood before the long black stove, remembering his life as a Tang Dynasty king. Now he fried chicken croquettes. The eternal Tao casts one up and brings one down, he reckoned, moving quietly amid his steaming, sizzling pots and pans.

The day manager was handsome, with finely sculpted face, prematurely grey hair, baby blue eyes. As movies were sometimes made in the neighborhood, he hoped he would be discovered and get to Hollywood. He did not speak too good English, but he was good-looking, for sure. On Sunday, his day off, he dined with an employee of the ladies' stocking shop next door, a woman of mature beauty who bore the faint trace of a number tattooed on her forearm. Sometimes they spoke, half-joking in the afternoon, of returning together to the old country.

The cashier at the desk beyond the turnstile smoked a cigar and made rapid change with an elegant flourish of hands. He lived alone in the hotel across the street and had no plans. On the way home, he talked to the butcher, and the butcher's cat rubbed against his leg.

The Chinese cook recollected his houses and his ladies in waiting, his palace in the moonlight. Small boats floated in the waters beyond the garden.

"Gimme a beef stew!"

"You betcha!"

The busboys wheeled carts around the cafeteria, filling them with dirty trays and dishes. They sang quietly and were far away.

"I even seen her eat off somebody else's plate!"

"No, Gladys."

"So help me, I seen her wait until this nice young man left his table and then she sat right down there and finished his leftover potatoes with gravy."

There were many soldiers at the cook's disposal when he was king. Where were they now, those soldiers?

© © ©

FIFTH AVENUE WAS BEAUTIFUL in spring. The leaves of Central Park bloomed and drooped over the avenue, and the moist, fragrant earth of the park was stronger than the fumes of bus and taxi. Julius Raker, retired owner of Raker Coastal Trucking Corporation, walked slowly up the avenue, toward his favorite haunt, the Metropolitan Museum of Art.

Retirement had brought Julius Raker up against himself, with nothing to do. Each day, he left his Park Avenue apartment and walked to the park, where he roamed, thinking things over, watching the children, the dogs, the clouds sailing above Manhattan. He wasn't satisfied; he needed a focus, as business had once given him. So he found the museum one year ago, by accident it seemed, looking only for a place to eat lunch on his round of the park, and discovering, instead, his soul.

He'd grown silent in his home, preoccupied with thoughts about time and stone. *Julius,* said his wife, *I'm going to Hadassah, do you feel alright?* From his window, looking out over Park, Madison, and Fifth Avenues, he could see the roof of the museum in the night, lit by round globes. *Yes, I'm alright, you go ahead.* The business, Raker Trucking, was done; the maps, the fleet of trucks had been replaced in his heart by vestiges of ancient cities.

He walked along the avenue now, and the great stone building of the museum became visible through the overhanging green of the park—a temple, a church, a dream.

He entered, not through the glory of the front doors, for the many steps there made his heart work too hard; he entered through the side door, into the basement, past the dull, staring guards, who saw none of the beauty. Raker saw it, had been transformed by it. Sixty-five years old, he felt ageless, or ancient, which seemed almost the same thing.

Riding the elevator to the main floor, he stood quietly, holding his hat. He walked past the museum restaurant; marble-topped tables lined a fountain pool, where naked men frozen in bronze ran across the water.

Turning, he was with the old statues of the hall-way—heavy stone men with shovel-shaped beards and absurdly broad shoulders, wrought in chunks. Man's childish consciousness had made these things, and Raker stood, childlike in their shadow, feeling a remote region of his unconscious stirring. Dim, stone-dead almost, but awakening now as he stood silent, the archaic traces of his nature returned to him. He heard the heavy plodding of ancient feet in the market place. Stone buildings rose up from the sand, lit by torches, guarded by lions. The past, a riddle and a song, swirled up in him, fairylike, glistening, and was gone.

He walked through a doorway of the hall, into Greece, going straight to *Amazon,* a creature of coarse beauty, one stone breast showing, the other covered in stone tunic, her great muscled legs walking along in the sunlight from the museum window.

In the warmth of the sun with the Amazon, Raker left his arthritis behind. His bent shape, tired from a lifetime of hauling a trucking company, flowed into hers, assimilating her firm stride and tireless grace, as his mind opened to the more elusive reaches of time. They walked together. Children played in the dust. Heavy is the load of stone which I carry through the ages.

◐ ◐ ◐

"I HAVE ADVERTISED for an ornamental hermit." Lord George Beaverboard, leaning an elbow on the mantlepiece of his huge den fireplace, struck a light to his pipe.

"No, my dear," said his wife with a sigh.

"I should like to see some old fellow hopping about the place."

"But, my dear," protested Lady Agatha, "whatever will you feed him?"

"Old bones, filthy biscuit," answered Lord Beaverboard. "I put an ad in today's *Times.*"

That afternoon, a number of odd callers disconcerted Lord Beaverboard's butler. An old tubercular was turned away with a ten-pound note. An insane Russian balloonist was ruled out. A middle-aged, lumpish man with wispy goatee seemed to have the position until he lapsed into an epileptic seizure, and was removed through the servants' entrance into an ambulance. This left Douglas Perky, an insolent fellow, apparently cheerless, as the favored candidate.

"But why should you want to be a hermit?" Lord

Beaverboard wanted to be sure before he installed the man in his garden. There would almost certainly be visitors from Parliament, and the hermit must give the proper impression. The grounds needed a touch of intensity, for lack of wild game.

"Yes," Lady Beaverboard chimed in, now quite taken with the idea, as she'd be the first to have a hermit in a dull season, "why do you want to be *our* ornamental hermit?"

"Balls." Douglas Perky lifted up the corner of his lips, exposing a line of irregular teeth.

"Eh?" Lord Beaverboard liked the sound of that, could hear it ringing across the estate, through the mists.

"My *dear!*" whispered Lady Beaverboard, giving her husband's sleeve an urgent tug, to indicate her firm disapproval.

Lord Beaverboard took Perky by the elbow and opened the French windows. "Shall we walk in the grounds?"

"My dear!" Lady Beaverboard flushed completely as Lord Beaverboard and his hermit-elect walked out of the great house, into the sweeping gardens.

There were fifty acres of ground on the estate, some wood, some field, some carefully tended hedges. "We've got just the place for you, I think," said Lord Beaverboard. "It's an old game hut."

Perky veered to the right, toward a culvert that crossed the garden. He stooped on the edge of the ditch which fed into it. " 'ere's where I'll stay." The hermit slipped down into the culvert.

Lord Beaverboard knelt beside him. What a find!

For a pound a week, a man to sleep in a ditch. "We shall bring your meals out, of course. I expect you'd like some stale bread."

"Steak, you mean," said Perky, "with trimmings. I'm no bloody starvationist."

Lord Beaverboard hadn't expected this. Still, at a pound a week, and the ditch, let him eat steak. Perhaps he might start to take it raw. That would be a show.

◎ ◎ ◎

"NOT WOUNDED BY WEAPONS,
Not burned by fire,
Not dried by the wind,
Not wetted by water:
Such is the Atman,
Not dried, not wetted,
Not burned, not wounded,
Innermost element,
Everywhere, always,
Being of beings,
Changeless, eternal,
For ever and ever." Associate Professor Alexander Montrose closed the leather-bound folio and looked up at the class. "That is the Song of God."

A hand rose in the class, student Merriweather, the concerned: "Will this be part of the exam?" He poised his pencil over his notebook.

Professor Montrose stared at Merriweather, wanting to kill him. Certain powerful Tibetan yogis had blasted into annihilation those who interrupted sacred ceremonies. "Don't worry about the examination," said Montrose.

The bell rang, ending the period. The students rose, flopping their books closed, flocking to the door. Montrose looked down again to his folio of Scripture and closed it, his eyes playing over the elaborate etching on its tooled-leather cover, of triangles hooked with triangles, making a complex star bound by a circle. He felt a presence at the desk and, looking up, met the thick spectacles of student Merriweather.

"Who did you say was the author of that poem?"

"God."

"Yes, but . . ."

"God is the author. That is official. Prepare yourself for the examination on that basis."

Merriweather bent over his notebook, wrote the single word "God" on the sheet of lined paper. Then, closing his notebook, he left the room without looking at Professor Montrose.

Montrose stuffed his folio and notes into a battered briefcase and abandoned the classroom, going into the hallway, amidst the flow of young people. He preferred being lost in a crowd to heading a class. Shuffling along, just one body in a stream of others, the innermost element came clear to him. But speaking of it, in front of them, he could not make it clear. For ten years he'd done everything he could to make his students feel it—knelt on the desk and made faces, held classes on the lawn in silence, swore, laughed, made himself ridiculous numerous times. "Blind, crippled or crazy, you can know this *Atman*," he'd once said, remembering too late the crutches of the young crippled man in the front row, who did not return for the second lecture in Eastern Philosophy.

The flow, the flow: young women, perfectly groomed, expensively dressed; young women, like wet spaniels, shabbily dressed. The young men were him, a hundred naïvetés ago. The flow, the flow: he stopped by the window, looking down at the white, snow-covered campus.

Fools pass blindly by the place of my dwelling

Shining, the snow reflected the sunlight. The dark trees rose out of it, bare, arms weird and skyward. Tiny figures made their way through the drifts. Montrose stood transfixed, feeling himself flung out the window, across the day, in the snow, the trees, innermost element everywhere.

"A bit of a trance, eh, Montrose?" The nasal whine of Professor Wurt Cravis jolted Montrose back to his shell. He turned slowly to his natty little colleague, who was smiling victoriously, as if he'd caught Montrose masturbating in the supply room.

"See any flying Tibetans out there?" Cravis went to the window ledge, made a great show of examining the sky.

"I'm just leaving," said Montrose.

"I'll walk with you," said Cravis. Professor Wurt Cravis had done his doctorate on a crank letter sent by Bertrand Russell to the *New York Times,* and he began now to speak about some subtle aspect of that letter, but Montrose wasn't listening. Approaching them in the hallway was a petite brunette, her breasts clearly moving under a knitted wool sweater. She carried a briefcase, was older than a student, and answered the look Montrose gave her with little smile lines at the corners of her mouth and eyes. A wave of desire contorted his stomach as she passed by.

". . . information sent out by a perceived object . . ."

Grey suit, white boots, and her eyes, with only a few million veils across them, meeting his.

". . . light rising from a page . . ."

"Yes, Wurt, I see." Montrose felt sympathetic toward his colleague now, remembering that Cravis was supposed to be unable to endure whistling of any sort. At the sound of someone whistling, he was said to clap his hands over his ears and run.

© © ©

REVEREND DEMPLE CUPPLEWAITE bent over his flower garden, eliminating a weed from that bed of bright ladies, his girls, the flowers. It was a sunny day in Tay village, and the Reverend was enjoying his puttering in the stones and foliage which had been the daily devotion of generations of preachers. Reverend Cupplewaite was the latest in the line of shy, unambitious clergymen who had landed in the sleepy village of Tay, by the mouth of the river Tay, an uninspired little flow of water which ran the mill and occasionally overflowed its banks in spring, drowning a cow.

The Reverend's wife, Louisa Stagger Cupplewaite, was dead. Her portrait haunted the mantlepiece in the old stone rectory, and the ghost of her efficiency still lingered in the cellars, in carefully labeled bottles of jams and pickled beets, which Reverend Cupplewaite did not eat, for fear of being poisoned. A mysterious fever had taken his wife and her celebrated pickling secrets one difficult winter, making of Reverend Cupplewaite a lonely figure, the object of many a girl's attention, especially of Sally Fifer's, for she was pushing forty and lived in her mother's house in the flatland.

Reverend Cupplewaite had his suspicions, but he'd had enough of married life, and so he tended his garden, with occasional thoughts of the obscure God. On this fine day of 1875 in summer, he stooped to adjust the stem of a rose. Slowly his fingers worked the spine-covered shoot. The village held its dream, turning it slowly, of pies and women and the river Tay. In amongst the thorns, the Reverend went expertly, arranging a more striking turn of the rose than its own yearning for the sun had accomplished. Like the rose, Reverend Cupplewaite longed for direct confrontation with the Light, hoped to be met on Tay Road one day and thrown out of the saddle of his complacency and, like the rose, be drunk with illumination.

Such romantic yearnings were not fulfilled. Lightning did not attend his sermons, and those men of the village who did—the odd farmer, the store-owner, the postmaster—were usually half-sleeping in the sunlit pews. The ladies of the parish took comfort from his shy gestures and gentle tones. His grey hair, his baggy black suit, his white collar, his dusty shoes endeared him to them, and now as he was bending in amongst the delicate petals of the rose, Sally Fifer came through the front gate with a chocolate cake.

She was a tall, pale woman with large feet, and her cakes were the best in the village. The gate swung with a creak and Reverend Cupplewaite stood up. Anyone might be there—angel, devil, the Lord Himself. Life, that afternoon, might change upon the instant.

The feet of Sally Fifer, in their longboat shoes,

came through the grass, her dress playing about her ankles. Up her slender figure went Reverend Cupplewaite's eyes, past her hands cake-holding, to her pale face with its half-frightened expression. He could not penetrate, did not divine the Supreme Being there, nor the ancient love a-walking in his garden.

"Good afternoon, Sally."

"Well, it's not raining," said the shy woman, wondering to herself why it was she could not talk to men in the natural tones her mother had, like little musical cookies. Her voice was a crust of stale bread, crumbling in her throat. Though it was summer, due to poor circulation her feet were cold, and on Halloween she always awoke to find someone had hung men's underwear and baby clothing on her washline.

"Let me take that, Sally." Reverend Cupplewaite, with a smile, relieved her of the cake.

She surrendered it, a gift unworthy of the preacher, whose wife had made such special jams and pickled cukes.

"I still don't have the knack of it," she said, softly.

"Yours is the best cake in Pork County," said the Reverend.

◎ ◎ ◎

"HAAAR! YE SON OF A WHORE!" Here's me spit fer Tay Road, son of a whore. 'Tis a snake, bitin' its tail. I pull me hay wagon and the snake, she go aroun' ferever.

Stones by the road, lucky buggers, sittin' on their arses, a-talkin' to themsel', low and slow.

Hay wagon, yer too heavy fer a man me age. I come ter the bridge. Wheels go a-bumpity. Some fellers thinks a river moves, but it's the bridge moves, an' I ride it acrosst the water.

Snake road, she goes on a-turnin' ferever, down inter the green land, a divil long way. The sky is awful broken. Pull yer wagon down the road, to the French feller's shack. He's standin' in the doorway, smilin'. Waves his hand. I waves me hand. He waves his hand, got plenty o' hands. Don't speak no English.

"Here's oats fer yer nag, you bugger."

"Tank you."

"Ever notice the sky aroun' here, comin' apart?"

"Tank you."

Pull yer wagon up the path. Git back on Tay Road. Poppa is by the stove shavin'. Poppa, looky how ye come ter me, through the sky, shavin' the clouds. I'm stuck on Tay Road, Poppa. D'ye think ye can help me?

Not a chance, eh?

The flowers is talkin' ter me. *Hello, dark man,* they say. Every Jesus thing is a-talkin', an' I hear it. I hear too Jesus much. See too much, see it all, a-comin' apart. Wagon heavy, Poppa's throat beatin'. Who's that screamin'? Jest a worm in the bird's beak. I see an' hear everythin' in the Jesus county. Make a feller blind and deaf. And I'm only two year old, sittin' in the dark room, havin' a dream. Haaar! I'll wake up any day now.

© © ©

EMPRESS CATHERINE OF RUSSIA, riding in her summer coach, laughed, playing childish guessing games with her ladies-in-waiting, but her eyes were often drawn out of the windows of the coach, for they were accompanied by the guardsmen of the Preobrazhensky Regiment, riding beside the coach on prancing mounts.

She was past the perfect hour of her beauty, but had reached the height of her passion. Outwardly, in the presence of the nobles of Russia and the great diplomats of Europe, she was the dignified despot, efficient, businesslike, shrewd and ambitious. Inwardly, in the privacy of her chamber, she knew deep desire and girlish confusion. A handsome guardsman seen from the distance of a palace window might suddenly find himself called to perform personal sacrifice for Her Majesty. Thus every adventurous young man of the military cherished a secret hope, for Catherine's close friends were rewarded, not only in the satisfaction of giving intimate counsel to the lovely Sovereign, but by promotions, titles, and gifts of gold snuffboxes.

The dust of the road rose up, tossed by the great wheels of the coach and the hooves of the spirited horses. Catherine fell into silence, her prominent chin in her hand, her elbow on the satin door-arm, and stared out the window. The trees and roadside flowers fell away in a stream of color. She signaled, for they were passing an open field, bright with sunlight, and she wanted to walk there.

The gold-banded coach pulled to the side of the road, the driver's man leaping to the ground before the coach was fully stopped and rushing to open the door of the carriage; the flash of a sword froze his fingertips on the latch. The Captain of the Guard, rearing on his charger, pointed with his sword to the risen dust of the road.

The guardsmen drew their horses off the road, dismounted, loosed the horses to graze in the field. The driver's man waited until the cloud of dust had fallen to the road. Then, his own youthful eagerness settled, he solemnly opened the door for Catherine, who stepped down, holding her skirts up, so that her beautiful shoes were free to meet the road.

She stood for a moment as her ladies climbed down beside her. Then, when they had straightened out their gowns, she walked into the fields where the guardsmen's horses were frolicking. The ladies followed, several paces behind. The Captain assigned the ring of soldiers to fan out around the Empress, at a suitable distance in each direction, to see that nothing came forth from the meadow to disturb her. For himself, he chose a high rock, overlooking the entire field, where he sat watching, with his own thoughts, of horses, women, war.

Catherine walked on, her gown trailing in the gay weeds. The meadow was perfumed, the sky cloudless, and everything around her shone in startling detail, as if it were the carefully wrought ornament in a crown.

A wild flower, small, white, like lace, swayed gently between two dark rocks. She knelt beside it, drawn by its delicacy. Bending closer, she examined the gold dust of the center, and between herself and the flower there passed some secret, of the feminine, the beautiful, the doomed.

She rose to her feet with a sudden flood of desire. The field, the flower, the gentle breeze stirred the empire of her emotion, so that she seemed almost to spin in a dance.

Upon his rock, the Captain discerned his Sovereign's mood. Quickly he climbed down to the ground, called for his horse, and rode at a quiet pace until he was near the Empress, where he dismounted and came forward, holding the reins.

"Captain," said Catherine, pointing to the ground, "do you see this flower?"

The guardsman stepped forward until he could see the small white blossom.

"I want a man stationed here," said the Empress.

The Captain, betraying no emotion, mounted his horse. Minutes later, the destiny of one of his men, Private Sergei Razamov, was changed and firmly fixed. On foot the young Private hurried to the place of the flower, his sword swinging at his side.

As he passed the ladies-in-waiting, who were playing in the field, he was red-faced, for they'd grown silent, and he was inexperienced. But when he came to attention before the Empress, he was pure white, perfect in stature and uniform, clear-eyed and ready to die. He was left alone at his post, while Catherine and her Captain, followed by the ladies in waiting, withdrew across the field toward the coach.

When the dust of the road rose again to the gallop of hooves, he was standing still as stone, and when the dust fell back, and the road was again silent, he remained that way. Only when the night came on, and he was certain no one was watching (as part of some test, perhaps, of his faithfulness), did he break his solitary rank, sit down on the ground, and ponder his strange assignment.

chapter 2

THE TURNSTILE of the Golden Cafeteria rang incessantly: it was the lunch hour, the tables were filled. Spoons, forks, knives, plates clinked and clattered. Beneath this was the low mash and rumble of mouths and stomachs, and above it were the voices of the countermen shouting, of local businessmen talking shop, and of the old guard keeping their post:

"I says to her, I says, *You shouldn't eat the food left over on other people's plates, you might catch something.*"

From the busboys' carts the dishes traveled into the kitchen and were laid in a pile, becoming a mountain in front of the dishwashing machine. Working his way through this mountain was a reformed alcoholic, who took the dishes and racked them up on the washing tray, placing the tray onto a conveyor belt, which carried them slowly beneath a steaming canvas tent where jets of soap and water washed them. From there they passed through a rinsing tent and onward, cleaned, to the end of the belt, stopping by the kitchen counter, where the cook and his assistants grabbed them, loading them with food and passing them out to the countermen, who added salad, rolls, and butter, and passed them out to the customers. The chain continued in this way, round after round. Food—like a chant, the sound of its creation, preparation, and passing—rose and fell, and rose again.

"I says, *Hah! You eat every scrap left, like a dog, I says.*"

"You didn't, Gladys."

"Didn't I? I give it to her, I did. Did you ever see the way she talks up to Mr. Jennikins, whose wife passed away last year, God rest her, and lives up the Majestic, has a nice little suite of rooms there, I hear, the poor man, with no one to look after him, and she's after him, but I warned him. I says, *Mr. Jennikins, watch out.* I didn't say no more, I didn't want to worry the poor man, but he knows someone's after him now. See how he looks around when he comes through the turnstile?"

The cook reached without looking for a clean dish. It was always there, hot and dry. He slid filet of sole, lemon-dropped and white, onto the plate, adding mashed potatoes and peas, and handed it out the window. In the pool beside his summer palace, goldfish swam, veil-tailed, iridescent. He had walked there often, thinking, planning the Dynasty. There was the sound of a one-stringed lute coming through the cherry trees.

"Gimme a leg lamb!"

"Okey-dokey!"

◐ ◐ ◐

WITH DIFFICULTY, JULIUS RAKER separated himself from the Amazon and walked on, past beautiful stone Greek boys with their penises broken off, past a crouching lion over which he ran his finger as he passed, walking on, into the room of Vesuvius, where the frescoes of ancient Pompeii were hung: bulls adorned with flowers, in molten red, reflecting the volcano. Outside a stately manor, a red kettle was boiling amidst marble pillars. The kettle would boil over, the manor would be drowned.

He moved into the Great Hall, where young ladies were selling souvenirs, tour groups were forming, and the weary were sitting on the long leather couches that lined the huge hall. On the wall, a Persian tapestry hung, woven with furious intricacy. Raker stared at the glorious web, the mind of Persia in incessant stitchery, a maze of curlicues in thread of gold and red. The spider of gold had woven its pattern, of a center spreading out and out. The spider of red had woven its complement, in and in, toward the center, and the piece was alive with hypnotic action. Raker in the web, lightly balanced on its thin fibers, was a Persian prince, covered in splendor. He had no longing for human contact. His soul, a fine tapestry, hung in silence, filled with intricate Time.

Ancient figures moved—bright elephants, black kings. Raker sensed the march of a tremendous caravan, slowly, across the deserted sea of infinity, sands and water mixed and blown, filled with human bones and jewels. He walked slowly out of the Great Hall, feeling the weight of civilizations in himself: Italian marble, Spanish wood—San Miguel in robes of wood —hammered silver women of the Andes dancing where pottery eagles flew. In a cool room with a stone fountain splashing water, early Peruvian gods disported. The curator had ordered tropical plants and strong beams of light. Clay horses and worn stone faces held the center of the room with potted ferns, and beyond were the glass doors of the museum offices, through which efficient women and a man in a pin-striped suit could be seen. With the drone of the humidifier was mixed the click of the typewriter—time flowing, time ticking. A secretary opened the glass door and walked past Raker, through Peru, trailing perfume. Raker Trucking had hauled perfumes and spices, rugs and dishes, fine cloth, crates of jewelry. He knew the world, knew women, had employed many secretaries.

© © ©

"DOUGLAS PERKY IS INSTALLED in the ditch!" Lord Beaverboard, in high excitement, returned to his wife, who was sitting at her charitable works in the drawing room of their manor.

"Who, my dear?" She had resumed her crocheting, making little fringe-end pillow cases for poor men in the slums.

"Our ornamental hermit!" exclaimed Lord Beaverboard. "He's living in our ditch."

"How disgusting!"

"It's just the thing to bring our party back to power!"

"Surely you're not going to support Mr. Porky for office?"

"Perky. No, of course not, but having him out there is bound to arouse public sympathy." Lord Beaverboard paced back and forth, reform bills tumbling through his mind.

There was discreet footfall at the threshold. Krabs the butler stood stone-faced in the doorway, though the careful observer might notice a slight twitch troubling his eyelid. "There is a vagabond in the old culvert, milord. Shall I phone for the police?"

"Serve the man dinner, Krabs. I believe he said he wanted steak with trimmings."

"Very good, milord." The twitch in the eyelid of Krabs ceased, the neural path opened again, and the servant appeared presently at ditchside with dinner, on a silver tray, covered in a silver dome, insisted upon by Lady Beaverboard, who did not want the wives of the Members of Parliament to think she treated her ornamental hermit like a servant.

"Hand 'er down, mate."

Krabs, though filled with loathing for the ruffian below, passed the tray with perfect calm, as silver in his hands brought out the high polish of his profession.

When night came on the ditch the ornamental hermit turned over in the dirt, quite comfortable, except for the stars, which kept him awake.

The following morning the hermit asked for a

shovel, through Krabs, who relayed the request to Lord Beaverboard.

"Shovel, is it? Let's have a look."

Lord Beaverboard, in tweeds, crossed his estate, to the ditch, where a pile of earth was forming on the edge. He peered over the mound of dirt. Perky was tunneling below.

Lord Beaverborad signaled to the silently waiting Krabs, and they walked off across the grounds toward the manor house. "The hermit is going to live in a hole in the ground, Krabs. It is this kind of spirit that has made the British Empire the Queen she is."

"Very good, milord."

"I shall point that out to the House of Lords, directly."

© © ©

PROFESSOR ALEXANDER MONTROSE returned to his office in the Old Letters Building. It was a small bare room overlooking the downward slope of the campus, toward the town. He sat at his desk, straightened his back, folded his hands in his lap. His mind continued to flow, scattering thoughts, arguments, ambitions, seductions. Slowly, as he watched his breath rise and fall, the stream of thoughts flowed around him, and he was a calm, silent stone in bright, sparkling water.

"Hello, Montrose, are you decent?"

"Yes, come in." Montrose remained seated. The figure of Associate Professor of Philosophy Robert Gash came into view. He was a large man, gave the lectures on Aristotle's Ethics, and had none of his own.

"I'm not interrupting?" He sat on the window sill, facing Montrose.

"Not at all."

"Getting any pussy lately?"

"Nothing to speak of."

"You underestimate the orgasm, Al. It's not healthy to hold in your jisom." Associate Professor Gash was a graduate of analysis in his underwear. "Loosen up the blocks in your balls. You've never had therapy, have you?"

"No."

"Have a chat sometime in your underwear."

"Did you say chat or chap?"

"Eh? There's nothing like sorority sister puss for genital flow. My blocks are removed."

"It's always a pleasure to talk to a liberated being," said Montrose.

"My balls are tingling," said Gash. "Women sense it."

"I've got to get to my next class." Montrose stood, picked up his briefcase. The two men left the room, entering the silent hallway of Old Letters.

"The President of the University is afraid of the orgasm," said Gash quietly. "I suggested to him that we begin a seminar in the orgasm. He went into a cold stricture."

"What would Aristotle think?"

"Aristotle was uptight about crude jokes. He wasn't getting any energy below the waist."

© © ©

REVEREND CUPPLEWAITE and Sally Fifer walked across the garden toward the rectory door, around which the ivy wound and tangled, giving off its faint green smell in the sunlight. The Reverend opened the door, and Sally went forward, stoop-shouldered and big-footed, stumbling, as she usually did, through the door into the kitchen.

A big fireplace yawned there, surrounded by pots and pans, neatly hung, dull black in the sunlight that streamed through the high windows and brightened the stone walls. Reverend Cupplewaite and Sally Fifer stood in silence for a moment, like divers poised above still water, reluctant to shatter its surface. Then they stepped, slowly, into the room, through the stillness.

"We'll put some tea on," said the Reverend, opening the lid of the wood stove and dropping a match into the prepared kindling. When it was flaming, he added a chunk of dry wood, scooped water from a large bucket, filling up a tea kettle of copper, which he placed over the heated part of the stove. Through the crack of the stove plate, the yellow flames flickered. He took two delicate china cups down from their brass hooks in the cupboard.

Sally sliced the cake, and they stood there, waiting for the boil, as the dust of numerous reverends rose and floated in the sunbeams, while over all brooded the jealous ghost of the Reverend's departed wife.

The steam rose in the kettle, bringing a smile to

their faces and a frown to the old ghost. The boiling water was transferred to a charming china pot, and it and two cup settings were carried by the Reverend into the sitting room, while Sally slipped the cake slices toward two plates, picture plates which showed a coach pulling up at an inn. A woman was waving out the window, and a small boy was hurrying to the horses, as the sun came through the painted trees warming the eternal figures, just before the chocolate frosting buried them.

© © ©

O THE TAY ROAD O

I got a pain in me shoulders like a knife, son of a whore of a wagon. Little pink flowers talkin' on the roadbank. *Hello, dark man.*

"Hello, little gals."

Where you goin' today, dark man?

"Jest down the road a-piece. I'll see ye later."

Goodbye, dark man.

"Goodbye, gals." Nice little gals. Don't do no harm. Divil got his knife in me back. I seen the Old Prick many a time on Tay Road. I talk to him, too, he ain't sech a bad feller fer talk. Scare you though when he come up outa the ground in front o' ye, big as the sky.

O the Tay Road O

Poppa come with his beard sa black. They said ye was dead, old man. *No, I ain't dead, son. I'm jist a-floatin'.* I cain't figure it out, Poppa. *What's the matter, son?* I'm all broke apart, Poppa. One part o' me head is up in the sky and another part in the ground. Sometime I feel meself spinnin' sometime I go up to the sun burnin'.

Pay it no mind, boy. We're all jist a-floatin'.

Poppa's face is a-breakin' up, into birds, into clouds. I'm comin' up ter Mister Whatsis's place. Got ter give that feller oats fer his nag. I see his face in the winder. Now he come ter the door, a white-haired feller, kinda jumpy, part beaver. He's a-wavin'. He's a-talkin'.

"Set them oats in the bin," he say. "The mare is got a real hunger today. We been plowin' the East Meadow."

I carry the oat bag, step inter the dark barn. The little birds scatter up high, the mare she say, *Hello, dark man*. She got a long face, sa sad.

"She was limpin' here last week, son of a whore of a Frenchman blacksmith put the nail of her shoe right into the quick." Mr. Whatsis lookin' mad.

I'm strong as twenty men, she say ter me, on the quiet.

"Well, she likes them oats, don't she?"

"She likes 'em fine."

He gimme a few cents and I git back ter the wagon.

"Why'nt you git a horse to pull that goddamn thing," he say.

"'Tain't fair."

"Fair? Why Christ a-mighty, man, what's fair in this world?"

I pull me wagon up the lane. O the Tay Road O

© © ©

CATHERINE'S LOYAL YOUNG SOLDIER stood
guard throughout the second day, alternating between
standing at attention over the flower and marching
around it. Between times he glanced at it, unable to
see what was special about it. The field was filled with
flowers, one kind and another. Why this one? Why
anyone? Why himself?

He marched, marking off a square around the
small white queen. He stood rigidly beside it, and flies
alighted on his brow. He sat, squatted, knelt by the
flower, got to his feet, and marched again. Of what
military plan was he part? War imminent? Some
meeting of diplomat and courier, of spy and contact, of
scout and sentry?

All morning he watched, all afternoon. He prac-
ticed his sword against the wind, ate the few provisions
he had in his small duty bag. As the sun began its second setting on his field, he cut pine boughs from a near
tree, laying himself a bed. Without fire, he met the
darkness. The field grew damp, cold. He crawled onto
his bed of pine, covered himself with his cloak. A last
look at the flower showed that it had closed up, too.
All was quiet. He slept, waking himself automatically
at midnight, when he rose and kept the first watch,
stretching beside the sleeping flower, peering across
the field toward the forest, then the other way toward
the road, searching for a light, a coach of horses with
muffled hooves, a statesman, dropping discreetly from
the door, an ill-favored courtier, led to the dark spot,

then misled, buried beneath the white flower. What? Why?

No light came, except the cold moon and stars. He waited, slept again, hungry and eager for the dawn.

chapter 3

EACH MORNING outside the Golden Cafeteria, an old woman would appear, riding in a wheel chair, pushed by a handsome old black man with grey beard. She came wrapped, heaped in rags, which covered her head like a turban, were piled on her body, flowed over the wheels of her throne. The black man's clothes were worn and shabby, but they were clothes. The sultana's vestments were old washcloths, towels, shirt tails, collars, sleeves, handkerchiefs.

His voice was deep, gentle. "Is you comfo'table?"

She nodded her head and raised her hand to adjust her headdress, revealing a thin, bony arm.

He parked the wheel chair outside the cafeteria, and she sat there, looking at Broadway.

"De sun bright today," said the black man, pushing back his battered hat.

The revolving doors of the cafeteria spun the sunlight as two of the old guard went through: "She ain't here yet, Gladys."

"It's too early for her kind. Nobody leaves nothing left over this time of day."

The black man bent down to the woman in the wheel chair, smiled. "De sun will make you better," he said and stood behind the rag queen's throne as the morning light beat down and, when it passed on, they followed it, along Broadway.

◐ ◐ ◐

JULIUS RAKER STEPPED OFF the museum escalator amidst the Chinese vases. They were silent, deeply so, within glass cases. Butterflies chased with wings of polished light; mimosa blossoms were attended by wise birds; a pavilion floated in the clouds, and ladies of exquisite manner set a tray on the terrace of the Commissioner of Royal Highways. A red sun hung above the pavilion, and a dragon's tail curved round the neck of the vase, sweeping upward to the mouth.

I have bamboo eyes. This terrace in the clouds, the winding road below—I have known them all before.

He felt shadowy memories, numerous cloaks and moods, not his, yet his. "The world is magic," he said, staring at a small porcelain figure of a Tang Dynasty queen, her hands clasped in white expectation, and she was in half-bow toward him. *Chang made me*, she said, in a shy whisper.

He passed through the glass, taking his place beside her, in the figure of the God of Wisdom, whose forehead was largely domed, and whose long porcelain beard of white was filled with curves, like the waves of the sea.

© © ©

THE ORNAMENTAL HERMIT WAS OUT of sight a good deal of the time, tunneling his home in Lord Beaverboard's old family soil. He had deepened his ditch to ten feet, at which point he struck off into a side wall, carving himself a doorway into the earth.

The doorway became a hall, shored up by beams of wood and lined with paneling, supplied by Lord Beaverboard, who did not want his backyard to collapse under the feet of the Prime Minister. Two men had been hired and put under Perky's supervision. With this added labor force, good for the nation's economy, the hermit's grotto home took rapid shape. The underground hallway led to a main room, approximately ten feet square and six feet high. It was in this room Perky now worked, speaking with his men.

Upon the surface, Lord and Lady Beaverboard heard muffled voices beneath them in the sod, but could not distinguish the words clearly. Lady Beaverboard tapped her dainty foot on the soil. "Is it safe, my dear?"

Lord Beaverboard gave the earth a good thump with the handle of his umbrella.

"It's most unusual, I must say." Lady Beaverboard peered into the ditch. "Like moles or something."

"The indomitable spirit of the English," said Lord Beaverboard. "It makes one stop and reflect."

"It makes for dangerous walking at night," said Lady Beaverboard.

© © ©

PROFESSOR MONTROSE SAT IN THE MUSIC Room of the Student Union Building, in a soft lounge chair, looking out through a large window, to the terrace, and beyond, to the campus, blown by March winds. Another semester had ended.

In the background, from the glass-encased listening booths, came the sounds of different records, blended together, cacophonously. Montrose felt a similar confusion in his head. He had nightmares each night, dreaming he was a student, that he'd not prepared his lessons for months, that he'd lost his books, forgotten the classroom number, the teacher's name, his own name, and was flunking everything.

Come now, Montrose, do you really believe all that Tibetan bosh? Myths, my dear fellow, pure and simple.

Montrose got up, walked out onto the windy terrace. The snows had melted into the ground. It was semester vacation, but he had nowhere to go. He thought he might be atrophying. His last sexual encounter had been with a town girl, a "townie," as they were contemptuously called by the student body. She sold tickets in the little glass booth of the movie theater, and Montrose, while drinking one night with two graduate engineering students, learned of their plan to drive out with her into the woods. They invited him along.

The girl was short, stupid, pig-faced, and reluctant to go with the three of them, but higher learning prevailed. Drunk, Montrose grew eloquent, in a foppish way, and made her laugh. They drove off in the night, Montrose and one engineer in the front seat, the girl and the other engineer in the back. After parking in the woods, Montrose and his companion engineer left the car for a while, then snuck back up alongside it, listening to the sounds within.

When Montrose's turn came, last, the girl was growing sensitive. The back seat of the car smelled of semen, but when he sat beside her she asked him what did he want and why didn't they drive somewhere for a hamburger and French fries. He tried higher learning again, speaking about time and women, and she asked him if he was a queer. Abandoning his monologue, he attacked her physically, and was repelled. Each repulsion by the girl rendered her more ugly to him, until finally, when she agreed to masturbate him in his handkerchief, playing dully with his member, it refused to erect. Later on, as they drove back to town, she asked the engineers why they'd brought a queer along.

© © ©

REVEREND CUPPLEWAITE WAS already sitting by the window of the sitting room when Sally Fifer came in carrying the plates of cake on a small silver tray. The window overlooked the garden, the flowers were open wide in the warm afternoon sun, and Reverend Cupplewaite was at peace. If only everyone could just sit at their window and be content. Here am I, and here is Sally, and the cake.

She set it down on a small round table, of polished mahogany, with slender legs, part of another century, as was all of the furniture which Reverend Cupplewaite had inherited with his post, and which the next shepherd of Tay would use.

"Perhaps this is as much Paradise as we are allowed," he said, smiling as he poured the tea. Jesus in the desert. Cupplewaite in the parlor. The cake awaited him. He would have two pieces and be satisfied as a flea.

The tea was sugared and creamed. A bee buzzed on the window and flew off.

© © ©

O THE TAY ROAD

She's a son of a whore fer turnin' and she never stop. She go down, aroun', and up, lads, and ye go down, aroun', and up wi' her. In winter it's Jesus cold.

Summer it's Jesus hot. Sometime not too cold, sometime not too hot, and that's where she have ye,
throwin' ye a nice day now and agin.

I pull steady, to keep me head from blowin' away
inter the sky, in little pieces puzzlin'. Some fellers sit
aroun', I cain't, I come apart. Part o' me go down the
lane, part hides in a tree. Here's Mrs. Whosis peekin'
out her winder.

"Hello, Mr. Jorgen!"

Chickens scatter in front o' her. Nasty little peck-
ers. I caught a partridge once sa nice with bright
feather and wanted ta keep her. Put her in the hen
house. One Jesus hour later I come back, and that partridge was picked clean.

"Not a feather left on her, they plucked her ta the
skin."

"What was that, Mr. Jorgen?"

"That's the Tay Road fer ye."

"Lucky we have you on it, Mr. Jorgen."

"Taint lucky fer me."

"The pony's so hungry, Mr. Jorgen."

Through the little doorway, I haul a bag o' oats.
There's the pony, starin' at me wi' his sad black eyes.
And when they pulls a wagon their mouth hangs open
from hard breathin' and ye kin see their red tongue
and their teeth, sa sad, it makes me cry.

"Mr. Jorgen, what's wrong?"

"Nothin', Mrs. Whosis."

"I remember your mother used to tear up sometimes, for no plain reason."

"Let's give ye some oats, boy, here ye go." Eats it
right outa me hand. I kin see in me head a silver road,
boy, and maybe you'll trot down it. It ain't the Tay

Road, no, God blast it! Hang onto that silver road, boy, it'll proteck ye from the cold.

"Here you are, Mr. Jorgen, a bit of copper."

Out of her apron, she give me the coin. It's sech a game, don't ye know? The goddamn Jesus bloody Tay Road give ye copper too, along wi' yer nice day.

"Goodbye, Mr. Jorgen."

Chickens git outa me way. The clouds still hangin'. Pull 'er on the road, boys, let's go. She stretches out ahead, wi' her dirt and mud. But I had a silver road in me head, a road turned silver. I'll walk a bit more, boys, maybe I'm ter find silver and gold. The Tay Road, she'll slip ye anythin' ter keep ye in harness. All the tricks, boys, I knows them all, from the start. We're here ferever, silver and gold. We're here ferever.

© © ©

ON THE THIRD DAY of his watch, the soldier of Catherine, with nothing to eat, fell into despondency. The day was warm. If he had the slightest bit of biscuit all would be well. He attempted to eat some small, sour red berries and held on, then, through the morning, by the flower.

Afternoon brought hoofbeats and a coach. When the lone driver reined in the horses, Private Razamov was at attention by the flower. He watched the coach door slowly open, and a white form, in many lengths of cloth, descended the steps of the carriage.

She paused on the edge of the field. The driver handed her a basket from atop the carriage. She took it, and entered the field. The coach was pulled over into the shade beneath the trees. The harness fell silent, and the only sound was the young woman's gown coming through the grass.

Private Razamov swallowed nervously. The young woman continued toward him. Long blonde hair fell out from under her bonnet. Her face was white, of palace delicacy, and her eyes were upon him, laughing.

She walked lightly, looking about the field. Both her hands clung to the basket handle. "I've brought you something to eat," she said, extending the basket toward him.

"We must be careful of that." He pointed to the small white flower.

Coming forward, carefully, to look at the flower, she knelt before it, providing Private Razamov an alarming view of her bosom, covered only casually by her blouse, and rather more definitely by some inner harness of white lace.

The Private came stiffly to attention, staring off across the field. He was young, new to the science of arms, completely uneducated in the tournament of love. His several hungers combined to produce a trembling in his legs and stomach, which he sought vainly to control.

The girl stood and then, spreading her skirts, sat, at a safe distance from the white flower. "Your Queen did not desert you," she said, opening the lid of the food basket. She was older than he, not by too much in some ways, by a great deal in others, and she removed a large cloth from the top of the basket and spread it on the ground.

Private Razamov knelt, adjusting his sword, then sat, as the lady-in-waiting produced fruit, bread, several bottles of wine, a large roast and two plates. "Oh dear, they have forgotten silverware."

Private Razamov unsheathed his sword and applied its gleaming edge to the roast, slicing it until it lay unfolded like so many pages of a book of flesh. He then wiped the blade in the grass and slipped it back into its scabbard.

"I suppose we can use our fingers," said the young woman and, picking up a piece of meat, laid it on her plate. "You must be famished."

"Yes," said Private Razamov, and he followed, laying meat on his plate and eating.

She smiled, ate daintily, he devoured, with stern manners, a good bit of the roast, followed by bread, fruit, and wine. When the meal was finished, the roast was wrapped carefully away, and the fruits and bread, though the wine was left out, and they drank another glass together.

"I hear water," said the young woman.

"There is a stream behind that hill," said the Private.

They carried the dishes and glasses across a small expanse of field and down a bank, through pine boughs, to a small stream, in which a trout suddenly darted, seeing their shadows on his sandy bed.

The young woman, taking care for her skirt, knelt over the water with the dishes and immersed them, providing Private Razamov with his second adventure in her bodice. Her white blossoms pressed upward, for she was bent forward on her knees. Sensing his desperate glance, she turned her head toward him quickly, catching his eyes in her own. Private Razamov looked away, staring at the exotic little mole on her cheek, and was unable to move.

She extended him her hand again. As he helped her up, she tripped, slightly, on her long dress, so that she came forward against his dashing uniform, into the unmistakable sword of the army. They grappled briefly. The birds twittered enthusiastically in the trees. Somehow, by some higher swiftness, her right breast came out of its harness, into the Private's hand.

The old trout came back down the stream. The shadows which had crossed his bed had fallen away; Private Razamov and the lady lay on the ground, upon the soft mossy bank.

Her white halter had completely faulted. She whispered, raising her lips to his ear.

He could not speak. He was just nineteen, his breeches flaming.

"Please don't take my dress off," she said.

Private Razamov, sublime confusion, attacked clumsily the buttons down the back of her dress.

"No, you mustn't," she said, helping him with the fragile holes, which she didn't wish torn. "Oh, you've undressed me," she said, as her dress fell away. Private Razamov was struck dumb by the sight of her underwear, a long white bloomer with countless ruffles covering her from knee to waist.

"If you must have these, too . . ." Putting off her relentless attacker, she lowered her bloomers, revealing her nakedness, except for a final curtain, where her legs met. The young soldier advanced his hand timidly over her belly.

"How quickly you've taken the hill," she said

softly and pointed to his uniform. "You mustn't get that dirty." He removed it in a frenzy, tossing it over a tree limb. Another branch, from his own trunk, was extended, and rising, toward the sunlight.

When her last veil fell away, she was blonde Venus in the sun through the pines, her stomach lit by a warm ray, until the shadow of the young soldier crossed it, and a more substantial beam of light fell upon her.

She taught him all the court secrets, helped him with his cannonry, steering it into position for the final assault on the hill. Before a shot was fired, she examined the balls, sighing in herself with the feel of them, almost weeping over the fragile mysteries of war. Then she brought the muzzle of the big gun forward and moved the mountain to it, so that cannon and sun forest met.

In the mountain was a cave, with an ancient growth of great delicacy drooping at its mouth. She gave him entrance and, sighing, slipped the cannon past the delicacy into the deep. Clutching her hands to his rear guard, she pulled everything together in the forest, making all the day spin in and down. The old trout leapt for a fly, swallowed it happily, went down to rest on the sands of his stream.

"Daring Private," whispered the lady and, rotating her hips, hummed the snatch of some court tune, very popular at the moment. The movement of her flanks caused him to fire cannon abruptly, with a gasp. She kept him in position, gave him time to reload, and then they resumed a tactic of pounding the hill, in brilliant waves of soldiering, until the mountain was flaming.

The birds became silent for a moment, for her deep hush swept the field in all directions. She was rising, it was everywhere penetrative, sweet victory, a picnic by the stream, a dream. Her breath left her, she touched the sky, rubbing her breasts against the sun, driving the ancient Venus wildly, shaking her legs in the air, kicking the young soldier softly in the rear as, finally, the sun burst inside her.

Catherine, ever the wise Sovereign, knew the tastes of her ladies—and of her military.

chapter 4

THE OLD WOMAN, much talked-about, came into the Golden Cafeteria in her ragged beaver-fur coat. Bent, prune-faced, friendless, she bonged her way through the turnstile. The sight of her set the tongue of her fierce adversary wagging.

"Look at her. She'll be stealin' somebody's dough-nut . . ."

"Gladys, it's Sunday!"

"I don't care. You watch her."

The old woman removed a tray from the pile of clean trays, added silverware and a paper napkin and joined the line of mid-morning breakfasters at the long counter rail. She passed the grapefruit and the milk, declined the main counter, where egg orders and ham orders and French toast and pancakes were being dished, choosing instead two bran muffins and a cup of tea. Leaning forward, crabbed in footsteps, she shuffled along through the tables, not looking at herself in the long mirror, choosing a table which afforded no reflection, but set alone near the kitchen, in the draft of meat grease and toast. She did not remove her black pillbox hat, nor her beaver coat. They did not seem removable.

She was out of sight of her adversary. She did not know the woman who hated her, or if they had known each other once and spoken, she'd forgotten. Most of her memories were gone, though occasionally isolated fragments of a childhood, perhaps her own, rose up out of the dark sea of her time and confronted her, like a slide projected, along with various spots, in front of her eyes. Passionless, she would watch, until the scene faded and dropped away: An old man in suspenders by a white picket fence appeared as she was setting down her tray, and the apparition held her for a moment. Feebly, she tried to associate herself with him. He might have been her father, or a stranger, seen perhaps as she ran the dusty road, rolling a hoop long ago, but she didn't know. She no longer knew who she was. She operated back and forth from her hotel room to the cafeteria, with an occasional stop at the drugstore, to fill a faded prescription, whose purpose she had also forgotten.

She placed her tray on the table and sat down in front of it. For an instant, as she stared at the heavy cafeteria silverware, a flash of her old identity returned, in the gay days of Prohibition in New York

City, with bobbed hair and brilliant smile, setting table for her guests, sportsmen, for her husband was a football coach, and they . . .

The memory dissolved. She stared at her silverware, unable to hold any longer the rosary of memory old women weave and finger hour by hour as time dies on and away. Her beads were unstrung. Was she that woman? Had she been a guest? Or the maid? She knew she was someone, a living thing that walked along and made the turnstile bong, whose echoing song told her she was there, had not passed away.

Bran muffins come with butter and jelly, and she applied her knife to the spreading of the jelly. Perhaps she had eaten food which others had left behind, but she had no cognizance of the act. Nowhere did it register, except in the heart of her adversary, the unknown conscience of the cafeteria, who even now was angling for an image in the mirror of the ghoul who fell upon castoff crumbs.

The bran muffin jellied, the beaver-coated woman opened her purse and removed a small vial, out of which she rolled a tiny pill, dropping it into her tea. Then, almost as an afterthought, she removed a small bottle from her purse. She shook it, held it to the light, then opened it. The bottle had a dropper which she filled with liquid. Holding the dropper over her muffins, she squirted the liquid, a few drops, onto each one.

She looked up, seemed to see something in the air: The hoop had rolled far down the road, almost out of sight, and the man with the suspenders had caught it for her. Then it was gone, and she swallowed one bran muffin quickly, whole, like a caged monkey. She rose, not touching the second muffin, nor her tea, and walked through the aisle of tables toward the door.

So unexpected was her maneuver that Gladys, her adversary, wrenched her own brittle neck, looking at the ragged beaver going. "Where's she . . . what's she up to?"

Bong

The beaver coat, the pillbox hat were out, into the street, past the window, shuffling, gone.

Gladys, agitated, rose, pirouetting uncertainly in the aisle of tables. She'd been prepared for a day of watching, and now one of her principal objects had vanished. Needing food to sustain her in the crisis, she walked trembling to the counter, ordering a glass of gaseous water and a package of crackers.

As she returned, she circled the tables, so she might pass the table of her departed enemy. She came upon it and, seeing the leftover bran muffin, stopped, shocked, horrified. The little brown muffin sat, perfect, untouched, on the plate. Beside it was a square of clean golden butter. Only the jelly packet had been defiled.

She moved like one in a dream, pulled by an irresistible magnet, or blown by a determined wind, toward the table of her hated. Stupefied, she stared at the bran muffin. Rage built inside her at the waste which was being perpetrated before her eyes, by that fiend in beaver. She laid her crackers down and her glass of water and sat, directly in front of the bran muffin. Suddenly, rapidly, she took it in her hand, bit it half through and, with rages of satisfaction, swallowed it down. Then, quickly, she popped the other half, too, and looked around, triumphant, ready to meet any eye that might have witnessed her righteous, dutiful act, which she'd done for God, herself, and the starving children of Asia.

Without warning, she felt a hand of inexorable power grip her from within—stomach, bowels, blood, and brain. She stiffened, her eyes rolled and, with a gasp, she fell upon the table.

© © ©

JULIUS RAKER REACHED THE END of the glass-encased Chinese vases and figurines, turning to his right, past the main staircase toward a small marble nymph in a water-filled pool at the corner of the hall. He stood before it, uncharmed, unmoved. It was a bad piece, weak, poorly felt, flat as soap. The little nude had none of the glory of the female form, no soft roundness, no delightful shadow. An unfinished artist had left her unfinished; a witless curator had purchased her; she decorated a corner badly.

His feet were aching. Raker Trucking, in the hands of his sons, was showing a loss on the West Coast. The doctor had showed him a suspicious cardiograph. He sat down on a bench along the wall and suffered. If only he'd started coming to the museum when he was younger and had strength in his legs! One of his sons had been arrested for transporting a ton of marijuana across the Mexican border in a Raker Truck. It had cost plenty to keep quiet. His other son seemed reliable enough, too reliable. The boy liked a lot of secretaries, liked to hold conferences. *I should worry. Listen to my heart. It's lost the beat. It's not the same no more.*

He sank like a stone in black water, through his

innumerable glooms, such as a man must accumulate, hour by hour, through the days of his life: embarrassments, failures, painful furies seemed bottomless. He raised his head, trying to escape them. From the corner of his eye, he saw the loveless nude which had precipitated his plunge. He couldn't do half so well. He couldn't saw a board straight, couldn't drive a nail. Who was he to walk through the museum, saying, this is good, this is not?

A flicker of sacred fire leapt in the temple. He felt its glow throughout himself. It was still there, burning, in spite of his woe. He closed his eyes and felt again the secret of the museum: Time was great, carried all beauties and lives, carried him on and on. He stood up, held fast to the illumination. The hall, the rooms, the treasures, were his.

I spent my life working like a dog for this moment. I can relax—no office, no job, plenty of blue chip stock.

At the far end of the hall, he saw a familiar figure—the statue of Brahma. He walked up to the stone four-faced god. In the forehead was a hole, where a jewel had been. A tiny fragment of the jewel remained in the hole and caught the floodlight from above, reflecting it back in winking colored light.

India danced before him, exaggerated, a dream, ecstatic. His mind was still again, solemn as stone, dead as stone is dead, the faintest movement of densely packed atoms. Let civilizations dance, and dance away, I remain.

A man and woman came down the hallway toward him. The countless ages are my inner nature. The woman was chattering, the man wasn't listening, I am a flame in stone, about her dining room, how it must look this color blue, of the china vase. Raker was drawn from his stone into her desire, tumbling from his station, remembering his own home—a town house, all wrong, in colors and furniture that brought no sense of this eternal time, winding, playing, creating.

Brahma's eye was no longer winking. He started to leave the stone presence, when he was suddenly possessed from within by an idea which brought a blush to his cheeks. He looked right and left. The man and woman had turned the corner, no one was in sight. Slowly, then, with hands clasped in front of him, he bowed from the waist to Brahma.

© © ©

THE ESTATE OF LORD BEAVERBOARD shook with explosion. Lady Beaverboard woke with alarm. The blinds were not yet open in her room. Had she been dreaming? She left her bed and went to the window. Drawing the blinds, she pushed the French windows open and, wrapped in her negligee, looked outward. Across the expanse of green lawn, she saw her husband and the ornamental hermit. The hermit had raised his arm in some sort of signal. As he dropped it, she saw her husband bend over, pressing down on a strange box-like contraption.

Warrrooooooommmmmmmmm!

Her window sill vibrated. A puff of dust appeared faraway on the estate. The ground seemed to rise for a moment, like water hit by the wind, then settled down again. She dressed quickly and proceeded downstairs. "Krabs, what is happening?"

"Dynamite, milady."

"In heaven's name!" Lady Beaverboard rushed out of the house and onto the lawn, going quickly toward her husband and the hermit.

"Lord Beaverboard!" She addressed him sternly in the formal, rising to her full stature as a woman of title, the first daughter of the Earl of Stomach-on-the-Glen. She demanded explanation for outrage.

Lord Beaverboard did not reply, was fiddling with the hermit over the little black box. "Damn me, Perky, the plunger is stuck."

"Patience, Yer Grace." Douglas Perky jerked the detonator upward and deftly jammed it down. The ground trembled beneath their feet, and a terrible roar burst upon Lady Beaverboard's ears.

"Good Lord!" she cried, clutching her husband's sleeve. "Have you gone mad?"

"That's got it, Perky!" cried Lord Beaverboard, wrenching his arm free of his wife's grasp and trotting off with Perky toward the scene of the explosion.

Lady Beaverboard uttered a whimpering cry.

"Keep the women clear of the trenches!" Lord Beaverboard dashed away in his field boots. Lady Beaverboard followed cautiously. Dust and smoke were issuing out of the miserable underground chamber, and she could hear her husband and the hermit coughing and pushing their way through the debris. She felt quite flushed. Trembling, her ears ringing, Lady Beaverboard withdrew from the field and entered the house, plunging herself directly, without breakfast, into her charity pillows.

Sometime later, Lord Beaverboard entered the house, appearing before her briefly in the doorway, covered with dust. "We've opened a new wing below."

Lady Beaverboard's day was dreadful. The afternoon continued filled with explosions. Finally, her stitches awry, she could stand it no longer. She rang for Krabs.

"Milady?"

"Krabs, please go and inform His Lordship that for the sake of my health and charity work this dynamiting must cease."

Krabs gave a perfunctory bow and withdrew. With sober, solemn, stiff march, he descended the stairs of the manor and exited by the front door. Above him, he heard Lady Beaverboard opening her casement windows. Beyond, across the lawn, he saw Lord Beaverboard bending over, his filthy hermit beside him. The hermit waved, shouted something. Krabs, descended from a long line of gentlemen's gentlemen, refused to be directed by the likes of such a blighter. He stiffened his gait still more, pushing forward, working in his mind Lady Beaverboard's order. He would give this hooligan the old heave-h——.

Waarrooooooooooooooom!

Lady Beaverboard, from her window, watched Krabs elevate in an eruption of dirt and stone. The butler rode the crest of the wave, tumbling stiffly in several loops and dropping, in numerous pieces, to the ground.

"I say, Perky," said Lord Beaverboard, as the dust cleared.

© © ©

PROFESSOR MONTROSE WALKED IN the spring night, performing deep-breathing exercises. Nothing like it for working out one's defilement. Then, with a sudden change of heart, he plunged into the cellar of the Tap, a smokey barroom. A three-piece jazz group was playing, and a black girl singing. He took a seat at the bar and drank beer, the only drink available to citizens of the college community. For liquor a man had to drive fifteen miles to the next town.

He listened to the girl's voice and the deep groan of the bass behind her, sinking into the blue mood of the bar. There were beautiful coeds all around, and he was afraid of them. They were superficial sorority sisters in the latest Paris fashions, or dangerous rebels, liable to parade naked in front of his apartment. He needed someone plain and sensitive like himself. The only one he'd ever met like that on campus was a botany professor. He and George had a sensitive evening, discussing with rare enthusiasm the cosmologies of science and religion, finding them agreeable in the fundament. Then, after several hours of high talk, George put on a record of jungle noises, turned out all the lights except for a tiny red one amongst the potted ferns, and chased Montrose around the kitchen counter.

I should have let him blow me.

> *Look at me,* sang the black girl
> *I'm as helpless as a kitten up a tree.*

It was the honorable thing to do. Instead I embarrassed him.

A voice at Montrose's shoulder made him turn. A vaguely familiar face smiled, introducing itself. "Axel Storm, Theater Arts. Haven't I seen you at Green Room tea?"

"Yes," said Montrose. "I was there once with a student of mine."

"Dreadful place," said Storm. "Don't you detest theater people?"

"I'm afraid I don't know much about them."

"Lucky for you. Can I buy you a drink?"

"Thanks," said Montrose. "I have to go after this one."

"She has a lovely voice, doesn't she?" Storm nodded his head toward the singer.

"Yes, she does," said Montrose, drinking up the rest of his beer. "Nice to see you." He gave a feeble salute to the theater arts professor and left the bar, going quickly up the steps and into the night again, cursing himself.

He walked along the street, trying to cure his melancholy with the sweet smell of spring, which only increased it. I've got no social presence. I insulted that fellow. Yes, but he wanted to blow me.

He noticed a slender figure, standing alone in a doorway. The boy flashed a smile. Montrose looked quickly away, walking on faster. Spring, it's spring, that's all. Many philosophers, men and boys, look at the Greeks.

Desire, in its many faces, pursued him, filled him, walked him through the night until dawn.

© © ©

REVEREND CUPPLEWAITE STIRRED his tea. The old things of the place filled him with peace. To be surrounded by good pieces of silver, wood . . .

"Sally . . ." He felt peculiar, felt the moment spinning. Hang onto yourself, Cupplewaite. Everyone in the village is watching every move. Nothing else to do. Sally looked up at him.

"Might we try some of your cake?" he said.

The moment passed, its components scattering irrevocably. Sally handed the cake plate to the Reverend. She felt quite dizzy. Was it her circulation?

Reverend Cupplewaite sat back down with the cake plate on his lap, looking at the chocolate granules and the creamy stuff between the layers.

Flies marched on the sunlit window. The Reverend turned to watch their delicate parade. The south window of the sitting room was bright, and the open screen brought the odors of the garden, grass and flowers. The flies went back and forth on the screen, rubbing their legs, watching with thousand eyes the day, hungry for the garden of delights. "If I let them out, a bird might eat them," said the Reverend.

He doesn't like the cake, thought Sally. He isn't eating it, he wants to feed it to the birds, and he sees my big feet.

"Well, let's try some of your famous cake, Sally." He moved his fork toward her chocolate heart. He stabbed her there with many points, erupting the cream, crumpling the dark walls, and took her to his mouth.

The chocolate-mouthed lover turned to her smiling, in the sitting room, in the sunshine.

"It's not all that bad today," said Sally, nibbling with critical tongue on the confection.

© © ©

O THE TAY ROAD

We go down here through the pines ta the camp. The boys been cuttin' a lot o' wood. I kin hear the trees screamin'. The others is jest waitin' fer the ax.

Feller down there, standin' in the door of the cabin. Rollin' hisself a cigarette. I'm comin' closer, he's a-lightin' up, a-blowin' smoke.

"Clear weather."

"So 'tis."

Two big birds, black and white, come circlin', come callin'.

"Here, Jack, Whiskey Jack! Here's a piece o' bread, ye blasted jack!"

Bird come a-hoppin' an' a-lookin', sideways.

"Come on, ye pesky divil, take it outa me hand."

Bird come up ta his hand, take a peck, flies away.

"Them jacks is friendly."

"O, they'll folly ye inta the woods and wait fer lunch."

"They folly the wagon, them jacks."

"Have some tea."

We go into the cabin, over ta the stove. I kin feel him livin' here, see what I mean? I go inta a person's skin. He pull a can outa the stove and pour the tea. His name, his name—John. "How ye doin', John?"

"Cuttin' some wood, Herman." He throwed his cigarette inta the fire. "How ye been?"

"I ain't gonna end me days on the Jesus bloody Tay Road," says I.

"Good a place as any. There's some pine boughs out there we kin drag ye under."

Moths laughin', fires burnin' inside them.

We drink the tea and then go out to John's horses, a chestnut an' a black 'un.

"Got to keep them fellers chained," say John. "Or they kick hell outa each other."

"Here's yer oats, boys."

We run fer miles together, dark man. They chased us through the woods.

" 'Member the time these two fellers got away on ye, John?"

"Chased those two sons of whores clear down to the swamp," he say, a-smilin', pattin' them on the side.

Pullin' me wagon on. Sky filled wi' women, blowin' in the clouds.

○ ○ ○

PRIVATE RAZAMOV WAS VISITED frequently by the young Countess that summer. Each trip she brought, in the arms of her coachman, load after load of food, enough to last Razamov through the warm months. The coachman joined them for lunch and wine and afterward returned to his coach for a nap, while Razamov and the Countess retired to the river bank.

She lay in the shallow water, rivulets of water cascading around her breasts, over her belly, down through the tangled golden weeds.

She dried her hair with a towel, and her breasts quivered; Razamov watched her, mystified by her flesh. The summer day was endless. Kissed there, and summer-swept, she, too, was happy. Such a lovely afternoon. She felt the stream of love trickling away as she stooped at the water. It had rushed at her with such a furious flow.

"How shall we remember this day?" she asked.

Razamov lay on the pine needles. She stood against a tree. Between her soft legs bare and parted, hidden in the golden hair, was the red mouth of Venus, of wet and whispering endearments. He stared, fascinated . . . that patch of hair, like a little yellow animal.

"Or won't you remember?" she asked, petulantly. "You soldiers . . ."

chapter 5

"I SEEN HER take the bite of cake," said an old man to the policeman standing above the crumpled body of Gladys. "Then she just crapped over."

Two men in white rushed in with an oxygen tank, bonging twice through the cafeteria turnstile.

"Forget it," said the policeman, holding up the bran muffin plate, on which a broken corner of the muffin rested.

The ambulance attendant smelled the poisoned morsel, wrinkling up his nose. "All right," he said, "let's get her out of here."

A stretcher with a canvas covering was brought in, and Gladys was placed in it. The cafeteria was strangely silent for a moment as she passed through the turnstile for the last time, and then the noises began again, of dished food, silverware, and the shouts of the countermen, calling orders. By the time the squad car arrived with a precinct lieutenant, the existence and whereabouts of the beaver-coated lady had been established. Several old women had watched the entire play, and were able to provide meticulously accurate accounts of the morning's drama. Though they did not know the name of the beaver-coated woman, they knew her hotel, had seen her pass through its doorway many times.

"Let's go," said the lieutenant.

"If she ate any of this muffin," said the first policeman, "she's stiff."

The police left the cafeteria, and a moment later their siren was wailing up the street, and those who knew what the next step was could hear its scream diminishing, not far away, at the Manhattan Tower Hotel.

In the kitchen, the Chinese cook was taking a ribbing from the countermen, who suggested the death had come from his use of too much soy sauce. He listened, half-understanding, but his English went little beyond the names of the various dishes he prepared. Yes, someone had died; the kitchen had stopped completely for a moment as the spirit flew, but now the work had resumed again, of chicken croquettes, made with bread crumbs and onions in batter and fried deep. They are served with white sauce.

© © ©

JULIUS RAKER ENTERED the European Wing of the museum, his eyes carrying him straight toward a pedestal, crowned by a glass bubble, inside of which was a piece of goldwork by Cellini—mermaid rising from a shell, a tiny creature of great beauty, with gold tail and miniature diamond earrings. Other minute jewels figured on her body, eyes emerald, nipples red ruby. Her tail curled into a gleaming shell of pearl, carried on the gold back of a turtle, whose eyes and fins were jeweled and webbed with silver.

Raker glanced furtively around, feeling the glass, as dark fantasy rose. This mermaid of gold would love being carried by a thief through the streets, to a decadent collector who would place her on his coffee table (stolen from the King's Chamber of the Great Pyramid, cursed, priceless). The collector's house is above suspicion. The mermaid remains there. The thief leaves for the tables of Monte Carlo.

Heart beating fast, he turned away from the sea creature as two young girls in tiny skirts walked past, with notebooks, giggling, their sweet legs beautifully shaped with new beauty, innocent, terrifyingly wise. Breath-shortened fever broke in his mermaid soul, and he followed the girls from painting to painting, as they took down names and dates in their notebooks, giggling.

He followed their laughter, their long swinging hair. They pranced, flaunting shyly knees and thighs beneath nylons caught in the shine of the art lights.

Bending here to read a name, they broke his heart.
Life!

The spirit of the museum made them giddy. They
sensed the delicate shade of beauty, of woman in wa-
terfall, and whispered secrets to each other, trivial
things pulsating with secret beat. On the surface noisy
girls, in the depths they were ancient sirens, calling
through childish disguise the ancient sailor.

He stopped suddenly, looked around, finding
himself in a room of old French furniture, plush ornate
pieces, stiffly stuffed and musty, and he felt his own
age, as his vitality sank. The young girls passed on
away from him, turning the corner out of the stuffy
room.

His wife, since he'd found the museum and returned from it each day with a dazed and satisfied
look, suspected an affair.

© © ©

DOUGLAS PERKY WALKED beneath the ground
in his new main room—a large, circular, central hollow, shored up with concrete pillars, the ceiling and
walls finished in wood paneling. The furniture, placed
by Lord Beaverboard, was solid Victorian. The rooms
were lit by soft electric bulbs strung throughout the ornamental cavern, whose size was several subterranean
acres of the estate.

"I say, Perky!" The voice of Lord Beaverboard
came through the long hallway, and a moment later
he appeared, in his smoking jacket and field boots.

"Evenin', Lord Beaver. 'ave a seat." Perky extended his hand toward a small armchair.

Lord Beaverboard hauled out his old meer-schaum pipe and filled it. "You've got the right idea, I expect. Get away from it all."

" 'ow're things in government, Lord B?"

"Trouble with Germany." Lord Beaverboard sighed.

"Is that a fact? I don't read much paper."

"You've heard of Adolf Hitler?"

"Can't say I 'ave, Yer Worship."

"He appears to be snapping off a bit of what doesn't belong to him."

"Givin' the bugger the boot, are we?"

"Yes, Perky, we are. He'll listen to reason, of course." Lord Beaverboard tapped his pipe out on his heel and stood up. "You're proceeding with a new spoke?" he asked, indicating another hallway opening off the large central room.

"The diggers will be 'ere tomorrow, Yer Grace."

"Splendid! Let me know when the dynamite is to go off, will you, old man? I'd like to be sure Lady Beaverboard isn't around. She hasn't been quite the same since Krabs was exploded."

Lord Beaverboard walked out of the main room into a long dimly-lit hallway. "No need to see me out, Perky. I know the way."

On the following day, due to a minor miscalculation in the size of the dynamite charge, the ornamental hermit blew the front porch off the Beaverboard mansion, removing with it the leg of the downstairs maid, Mrs. Lickey, who was dusting a stair knob at the time.

© © ©

PROFESSOR MONTROSE STOOD in the doorway of the Dean of Arts' dining room with a drink in his hand. It was the Dean's semiannual sherry party. The floors were polished hardwood. The furniture was colonial. Vivaldi was played in the background. The assistant to the Dean, Mr. England, wore a toupee. The women, many of whom were over forty, had the grace and strength of their years on campus and did their best, wearing sheer cocktail dresses and talking enthusiastically of the latest sex reports.

The Dean had several original paintings on his walls. His library was old and went from floor to ceiling. Montrose walked from room to room. The women circled, like planets, round the central suns—the Dean, Mr. England, the senior professors.

It was afternoon. Montrose sat on a window seat, beside an original carved wooden Indian, who held out a handful of wooden cigars in the Dean's den. He was being eyed by Mrs. Winters, wife of the Head of the English Department, Dr. Sidney Winters, who was doing his Medieval English voice in the living room, speaking, just now, as the Wife of Bath. Mrs. Winters sat in a chair opposite Montrose. They were alone in the den.

She was dressed in a short party outfit of many black veils. Her knees were showing, and one leg was going up and down, crossed over the other—a sure sign, so Montrose had been told by his colleague Professor Gash, of her gathering lust.

The wife of Economics Professor Wright entered the room. "Is this a private affair or can we turn it into a *ménage à trois*?"

"Come in, dear," said Mrs. Winters. "Maybe you can get Professor Montrose to say something. I believe he's in a trance all the time."

"Professor Montrose," said Mrs. Wright, "I think religion is divine." She wiggled next to him on the window seat. "What is the position of women in India?" she asked, punctuating her sentence with pressure of her thigh on his.

Mrs. Winters' leg fairly flew. "My dear, haven't you ever seen an Indian temple?"

"Professor Montrose," said Mrs. Wright, "do you think you could teach a fatty like me to sit cross-legged?"

Montrose felt peculiarly unwholesome. The aura of the ladies was like that of an amoeba swallowing its prey. They were soaking up his vitality, flirting to flatter themselves. Beneath their perfumes, he smelled a closet, filled with old disguises. He took leave of them, to chew over him, two bitches on a bone.

The sun struck him as he entered the living room again, and he felt in rapport with it, above the sherry clouds. He felt, too, the impossibility of communicating his heart, which dreamt itself one with the sun. He left the sherry party, quietly, by the back door, through the Dean's garden.

◐ ◐ ◐

REVEREND CUPPLEWAITE CHEWED with mounting delight the soft flesh of the chocolate cake, as the dark icing of sugar found its way into the delicate portals of his tastebuds. Sugar, thought the Reverend, swallowing the mouthful of cake, juicy sugar.

Sally Fifer could feel his delight, it made ripples in the layers of her mind, but passed quickly, as the distance between them dawned again. She was a footstool away from him, and never had they touched, save through cake in the afternoon.

Reverend Cupplewaite opened a button on his black parson's vest. "Well, Sally, and how's your mother?" he asked, filling up the vacant space between them, so as to take her attention away from his devouring of cake. A minister of God must not appear the glutton, no. A family canning project, a boy's whooping cough, perhaps, while I take just the slightest nibble here, of the chocolate.

"She's well," said Sally, slumping in her seat, oppressed by the weight of Mother's existence. She felt that efficient lady in herself, overwhelming the scrap of personality that was her own. There was a lovely patterned rug on the Reverend's floor. She went to it with her eyes and heart, fleeing from her mother's presence. "Is that from Arabia?"

"Why, I don't know," answered the Reverend. "It does seem ornate."

The minarets rose up from the weave, beguiling Sally and the Reverend with hot thoughts and cobra-shaped notes from a long thin horn. They passed together into the flame of ancient burning. "Yes," said Sally, wiping a wisp of hair from her brow, "it is awfully . . . twisty."

One must eat cake like this with the slowest of forks. I must stretch out my days, Lord, of service to You. The Reverend aimed the four-pronged instrument at the dark mass and slowly brought it down, removing, like a sculptor, a small corner of the cake. "And your brother, is he still helping Mr. Tit with his pig barn?"

"Yes," said Sally, crossing her legs beneath her length of dress. "Hank says they all squeeze into a little space together, like sausages."

"Why, yes," chuckled Reverend Cupplewaite. "That's what they are, isn't it? Sausages? Cooking on the stove, crackling, with an egg beside them."

"I guess so," said Sally.

"All God's creatures have their assigned role," said Reverend Cupplewaite. "We must accept the miraculous working of nature, which doth provide." Sausages in the morning, with a generous sprinkling of pepper on the egg yoke. In the evening pork chops, crisply done. Hundreds of them, stuffed in there together; they must like the bodily contact.

"Poor little pigs," said Sally sadly, not looking at the Reverend, but flying to the fat camp of the pigs and huddling with them.

"We know that animals have no soul, and were meant to serve man," said the Reverend. May I have just the smallest serving of pig's feet, thank you, not too much. Sometimes, if pickled improperly, they produce indigestion. "It's right there in Scripture, my dear."

"Yes," said Sally with a sigh, "I suppose so."

"You mustn't trouble yourself with such thoughts." This is Paradise in the long afternoon. "Have another piece of your delightful cake. It will cheer you up, and I shall join you."

The flies buzzed up and down the pane. Reverend Cupplewaite relaxed more deeply in his chair.

The narcotic of chocolate was producing the lovely sweetness in his whole body.

© © ©

O THE TAY ROAD O

Ye jest go along. I never catched no rabbits, ye cain't blame that on me. Little bunnies go their way, and me, what's me name, Herman, I go my. Ner killed partridge. Ner set the bobcat trap, CLAP, with iron teeth on yer fur paws. Never went huntin', no never killed nawthin'.

"O, Mister Jorgen!"

I hear girl's voice a-callin'. Where she be, I'm a-lookin'. Apple tree, there she's swingin'. She young ain't she, with her skirts a-blowin'. Clouds come down, white in her skirts. She swing up the sky an' in the apples.

"Mr. Jorgen, my father wants some oats."

"Who's yer father?"

"You know, he's the doctor."

Pull the wagon around, now I remember, the horse is in the back.

"I ride the horse now, Mr. Jorgen."

She's right close by, and when I married her she was young. I can smell her now, leaves and berries. I strong as the bull, quite young mesel'.

"I've ridden him all over the meadow." She open the door and he the horse in there dark eyes me. I don't ride 'em, ner ask 'em ta pull me down Tay Road. Tain't right, O the Tay Road.

"Well, then, here's Mr. Jorgen. Hello, Herman."

Well then my head is a long time goin' aroun'. There her face an' apple tree, now sky cloudy women all a-goin', now he, doctor white shinin'. I've seen the feller fer years, uster run with him in the Tay Road, hell-fer-goin' in the sun.

"How are you feeling, Herman? That wagon's not too heavy, is it?"

"What wagon?"

"You know very well what wagon. You're about ready to retire, Herman."

His face smilin' frog. Why that tongue could reach ta the next county. With that instrement he listens yer heart. I listen the trees, which have no heart. Git back ta yer wagon, before these nice people do ye harm.

"Mister Jorgen, wait!" She runnin'. "Here's your money."

"Thank ye." Herman has a pocketful o' pennies ta weigh him down along Tay Road.

"Why not come in for a checkup, Herman?"

Pick up this cart now, make tracks down Tay Road. Look at 'er flashin'. She's worked up, boys, throwin' me snakes. I know 'bout young an' old, 'bout trees, an' Tay Road. The poor divil of a doctor don't know he's a slave o' Tay Road, wi' his horse pullin' 'im. The long low Tay Road goin'—ye snake divil road, I've not mistook ye fer a nice thing ta bring men pleasure. Some says, *It's jist pleasure ta take a ride.* No, I saw ye, an afternoon in summer found yer black skin shed on the road, and saw ye ripplin' on beyond it, one skin an' another. I won't be comin' in fer no checkup, no sir.

© © ©

WINTER CAME to the field of Catherine, covering the roof of the crude lean-to erected by her faithful guard, Private Razamov. The Captain of the Guard came also, with three other guardsmen of the regiment.

"We have brought your winter quarters, Private," said the Captain, dismounting, as one of the horsemen threw down the roll of a tent. "A store of food is on the way by wagon. It must last you all winter."

Private Razamov felt his heart sinking in the snow. He had been certain that with the coming of winter and the dying of the flower he would be freed from his post, to return to the regular army, to the men and the barracks, to smoke and laughter. As a man who has a sudden vision of his own death, he saw the long winter, brutally passing over the field, himself within it.

His emotion passed clearly across his face. The Captain asked if there was anything else he wanted.

"Smoke and laughter, sir."

"There will be tobacco in the stores, I'll see to it. As for laughter . . ."

But Private Razamov was already laughing, at the most incredible joke, himself, selected out of an entire army, for this, the flower.

The Captain and the guardsmen joined in the laughter. So Razamov was not unaware of the merriment he gave rise to in the barracks. Well, he's a good fellow, then, isn't he, not to take the thing too seriously. The dead, hollow field rang with laughter, which continued as Razamov's great tent was laid out and raised. It was a field campaign outfit, with room for a bed, a writing table, a locker, and closet. ·

The men raised the tent and then relaxed around a small fire near the door, talking as men-at-arms of glory and death and the women on the way to both. None spoke of Razamov's lovely visitor. Always it had been the same coachman who brought her, an old fellow, not part of the army. Razamov felt the court secret, then, with odd colors flying over it.

"Well," said the Captain, "we must be returning." He and his men left the tent, rose up on their horses, seating themselves high against the grey, snow-blown sky. The Captain saluted, spun his horse quickly, and they rode off across the field, their capes rising out behind them, red beneath black, free and gay.

chapter 6

THE KITCHEN of the Golden Cafeteria learned that not one woman, but two, had died, the other old woman having been found up the street, dead in the lobby of the Manhattan Tower Hotel, in a chair by a potted palm. The desk clerk had noticed nothing peculiar, thought she was napping. The story was carried back to the Golden, by those old women who had followed its unfolding, traveling up the street in their black shawls and back down again, bonging through the turnstile with loud lament.

Down the counter the story went, from soda-man to salad-lady, into main dishes, and back to the kitchen. The news did little to affect the efficiency of the kitchen; the kitchen men were impervious to most external sounds, except those orders which were shouted back to them and which they filled in the awesome voidness of their kitchen mind. When the murmur of *two dead women* passed through the cooking arena, the second cook thought for a moment, trying to fill the order: Two Dead Women. He surfaced and looked out through the serving rectangle which united counter and kitchen.

"Two old broads poisoned," said the coffee-and-bun man.

"Is that a fact?" The second cook felt strangely vulnerable in the outer-world stream.

"On a bran muffin," said the bun-man, holding up one of the small brown breads.

The second cook shook his head and returned to the stirring of his peas porridge, adding water to the dark green mash, and seasonings, turning over in his mind the dish of Two Dead Women. And then the meal was through him, and gone, and he was back in his green sea, in the deep bubbling pot.

The kitchen cooked on—onions, peppers, potatoes, meat, in shining metal, in dark iron, in hot oil. First cook, the Chinese, went from pan to pot, with his several spatulas, turning, stirring. In the palace women had poisoned themselves, for love, always for love.

"Gimme a beef stew!"

"You bevcha!"

© © ©

JULIUS RAKER SAT down on a leather couch in front of the painting of the harvest by Brueghel. The field was golden with cut hay, and the hayers, doll-like men in stiff-armed relaxation, sat over a basket of food. Far below was a village; nearby the steeple of a church. The peaceful scene filled Raker with calm again, and he studied the painting, losing himself in its detail, becoming aware of a strange thing: the hay-stacks, the way they were bundled at the top with cord, the way they spread open at the bottom where they rested on the field.

Then he saw the hidden element in the painting, and it brought him off the couch and straight over to the canvas, so quickly that a guard came directly over. "Don't lean against the rope."

"Look here," said Raker. "I'll show you some-thing incredible."

The guard moved toward Raker, suspiciously. He studied, not the painting, where Raker was pointing, but Raker himself, sizing him up for possible trouble.

"These haystacks," said Raker, "are shaped ex-actly like *paint brushes.*" He turned to the guard. "Brueghel himself was not conscious of that, I'm sure. Do you know what that means?"

"Don't lean on the rope, Mister."

"His brush, at which he was constantly looking, got itself into the painting without his knowing, right before his eyes. Look how those haystacks touch the field and spread open, one after another, like brush strokes." Raker's voice fell softer, drawing inward. "Brush strokes, you see."

"Yeah, move on now, please," said the guard, his own voice calmer, for he saw that Raker was just a harmless old nut.

◎ ◎ ◎

"ADVANCE, BRITANNIA!"

A jubilant shout rang through the underground home of Douglas Perky. The ornamental hermit raised himself up off the couch from where he'd been counting the cracks in the concrete ceiling. Lord Beaverboard, clad in military uniform, appeared in the doorway of the inner chamber.

"My dear Perky, we are at war. I have just returned from the House."

Perky opened an old French wine vault, removing a bottle of vintage champagne, part of a special store laid in by Lord Beaverboard.

Lord Beaverboard accepted the glass of bubbly.

" 'ere's to Adolf 'itler," said Perky, raising his glass in the air.

"Damn me, Perky, what do you mean?" asked Lord Beaverboard, withholding his glass. "Adolf Hitler is the enemy. I give you the King!"

They clicked glasses. The champagne was drained. "Well, I must be going," said Lord Beaverboard. "Holland and Belgium are falling."

Dynamite became more scarce with the war effort on, but the ornamental hermit, who knew a man in the coal mines, managed to secure enough to destroy the Beaverboard family vault, which exploded in a shower of skulls and then sank beneath the ground. The tumbled stone of the vault made excellent support for the walls of the hermit's chamber, and the skulls were placed as ash trays in his study.

© © ©

PROFESSOR MONTROSE SPENT the last afternoon of the semester vacation idling in the bookshop. At five o'clock he would register his students for the new semester, and the Great Wheel would carry him on for another round, the thought of which filled him with depression. He had no hope of lighting the flame of Brahma in the mind of youth. He had no hope of getting laid. He had no hope for promotion, as his colleagues thought his philosophical interests fanciful Tibetan bosh.

He entered the Corner Room restaurant. Estranged from faculty life by his tastes—when it was learned he was a vegetarian, dinner party invitations slowly ceased. His nibbling on the salad only, while others devoured rare meat, made them feel, shall we say, uncomfortable.

He chose a small table by the window and slouched in his gloom. He had failed as a teacher, flunked as a lover, fallen behind his colleagues in the climb to the heights of academe, and their wives wouldn't feed him brown rice. These failures were little enough, perhaps, but they contributed to the Great Failure—his inability to gain *samadhi,* complete absorption in the divine.

"Would you like a menu, sir?"

Pretty waitress, this. Bending over a bit to wipe the table, blouse falling open. I should like to be fully absorbed in her. "Cheese sandwich, please. And a bowl of vegetable soup." I don't hate myself, no. I'm a somewhat nice person at times, and I've seen the divine fireflash, once, twice. One night alone at the football stadium, clutching a bottle of white wine and wandering over the dark deserted field, across the faint yard lines, the fire of my soul flamed up, and I knelt in its heat and embrace.

Other nights, as sleep is coming, I see for an instant an ancient chandelier of candles burning, more brilliant than the sun, and that is *Atman* burning. I see it now and then, yes, and it is my grace, but I am caught in illusions of success and love, waitress approaching with soup, setting down bowl, bowls there in her white uniform, turned-over teacups, rice bowls perhaps, white soft, well then.

He ate, laying slices of pickle within his sandwich. The day passing by, out the window, the bright gods turning.

The Woman! Yes, definitely.

Montrose slid to the window, watched her walking past the bookstore, the petite brunette of the Old Letters hallway, dressed in trench coat, a thin briefcase under her arm. Wearing a beret, an existentialist perhaps, walking head down, in thought about the facts contained in the briefcase. I must leave my cheese sandwich.

"Check, please!" Urgent. Most pressing engagement. Her legs are in pale stockings, going. Muscles in the calves exactly what I need. Must act now. Large campus, lose her again for weeks, months. I am Shiva, thousand-armed, Lord of the Worlds.

He rose with his check, briefcase, went to the cashier, then through the revolving door. The street is grey. She has crossed over.

He followed her through the main gates of the campus, with reluctance. His clumsiness must enter, he could not avoid it. He must be self-conscious; *aham-kara,* the ego-making faculty works overtime in pursuit of the fair sex. And so I must die a little in the afternoon light. Still, in the realm of illusion, what is lost?

She was small, her waist drawn in by the belt of her trench coat. Beneath her beret was black hair, length indeterminate, caught up in some sort of top-knot, perhaps, with studied twists, of course, though made to seem casual. Trench coat essence of the boulevard at evening. *Pardon, mademoiselle.* Pity no rain, might open umbrella if I had one. What then, what?

In a few more strides he would overtake her, not wanting to, but forced to, because of the play of street and window and imperious gods, because he was a lonely scholar. Some part of him held back, even to the closest moment, remaining disincarnate, not part of his driven will. Still barely conscious of that mysterious witness, who played no human nor godly game, he drew directly alongside her and, with a word, lost all contact with the shining void, falling deep in evolution, chasing her mysterious reflections.

"Good afternoon." After all, I'm not a sophomore in sociology, but a man in his late thirties, with definite ideas.

She turned her head, amused even before she saw him. When she saw he was not a student, she was surprised, but not completely.

Close up, he saw her dark eyes and brows, red lips, traced only slightly by make-up; and ancient sadness rose in him as he looked at her and became for a moment the old scholar who knows better, and she, sensing the crisis, arranged a wisp of her hair, taking it from her forehead and laying it along her ear, with delicate fingers.

Montrose wondered what to do. With women he was an incredible fool. "You have remarkably well-shaped calves."

She looked quickly at him, her eyes flashing dark remarks, untranslatable so human were they, so original.

"Have you ever studied buildings?" Montrose pointed toward Old Main, ahead of them. "Not the grand ones, so much, but the dull ones. I am thinking of the bookstore on the corner."

"Are you playing a game with me?" Now she was sad, for they had touched in the afternoon. Men are so uncertain, rarely know when they've loved.

Montrose, himself now sensing crisis, was bewildered. No good to return to her legs. Impossible to share my building fetish. What then? Walk, remain silent, dissolve into the innermost element.

She too was calculating infinite distances, trying to determine by how much they were separated.

"Where are you going?" he asked.

"I have research in the library."

"Subject?"

"Topology."

"Study of tops?"

"It is the most beautiful of the mathematics."

"You speak to me from afar."

"There's the library," she said, stopping, ready to follow him.

"I left a perfectly good cheese sandwich to follow you," he said. "Have you had lunch yet?"

"No," she said and followed him.

◎ ◎ ◎

REVEREND CUPPLEWAITE FELT HIMSELF
slipping over the edge of waking, into the abyss of
slumber. The buzz of the flies remained in his consciousness, along with the outlines of Sally Fifer's body
in the chair beside him. He had ceased to recognize
her, or himself, or the sitting room of the parsonage.
The day seemed vast now, not held by boundaries,
contained neither in the church house, nor in bodies.
He heard voices—the beginning of a dream from his
forgotten childhood in the sun. The window was blazing; as a boy he'd seen a picture of the Taj Mahal, and
it rose up now, enchanting his brain with white marble. The flies droned lazily. A woman's lips moved.

". . . sugar . . . water . . ."

He swam in the sun of India. The day stretched
out in patterns of the lotus, the sky was flowers. He
broke the surface, dripping with beads of water. She
walked by the edge of the pool and turned.

". . . of course, Mother's oven . . ."

He drifted out and away. His head was heavy. He
was going down.

"But I said, 'Reverend Cupplewaite said . . .' "

His clerical training reached out across the waters
of the dream and gripped him. "Yes?" He sat straight
up, wiping deftly a drip of spittle that had formed at
the corner of his mouth.

"Well, you did say that Christian charity meant
remembering your friends, didn't you?" Sally Fifer
sipped her steaming tea.

"Yes, naturally . . ." Reverend Cupplewaite felt the tension leaving again, and the wave of sleep came once more. With one's wife, there was no problem, one simply fell asleep. With strange women, there was decorum, the duty of the office. I am a public figure, a man of God. A bit of tea will revive me. Is death a sleep and a dreaming?

"So we made up turkey dinners for all the elderly people in the village," said Sally.

"Yes, commendable." Reverend Cupplewaite lifted his eyes to the tapestry of the unicorn which hung in the sitting room, of the white horned beast, encircled by a fence. Something tragic in the weaving, he'd always felt it, that the beast should be found and trapped. The white body of the horse creature . . . the white blaze of the window . . . a most peculiar afternoon, thought Reverend Cupplewaite, as if the secret were about to disclose itself at every instant. Surely, there is a secret.

"Hammond Jackson said he didn't eat a thing all day, waiting for his turkey," said Sally, her cup clinking in her saucer.

"Excellent turkey," said Reverend Cupplewaite. "The stuffing . . ."

"Mother's stuffing has always been considered the finest in Pork County."

Reverend Cupplewaite kept his eyes on the tapestry. The dogs that barked there were disconcerting. What was the unicorn, to be so trapped?

"A stuffing handed down through many generations is a treasure, Reverend, don't you think? Just like any other heirloom?"

"Oh, my, yes!" said Reverend Cupplewaite.

© © ©

O THE TAY ROAD O

I'm sittin' in the road. All the gals is swingin' inter the sun. I'm blowed all over the county, I'm the wind, wheeee, liftin' the gals. The sands say ter me, *We all been kings, dark man.*

Sometime I'm a king. Me crown is made o' leaves. Me robe is made o' flowers. I was a king there one day, and they chopped me inter bits and grinded up me bones. None o' them sons o' whores could put me ter-gither again, that's why I'm sa blown apart.

The field is swingin' inter the sun. Looky the little butterfly a-goin'. May I marry wi' ye, me goldy bug?

The crow go by callin'. Death bird. Pick yer eyes out. Helluva way I'm in, all blowed out. Me head's over in the next county.

I'm tellin' ye, boys, I know the name and tongue o' every Jesus thing that moves. Caterpillars talk to themsel'. I never stepped on a-one o' them. The Lady in the Sky told me not ter squash them. O, she's bright as glory. She's tryin' ter fix me up, so's I'll be not sa crazy. Yessir. I'm gonner be a tree!

Time ter git movin'. The Tay Road don't ye know.

I know this place, this is the spot where Jimmy River fights the black bear, by Christ, let's watch 'er. Always he fights 'er, right here. There go the sun.

It's black as night. Here's Jimmy River walkin' along. Comin' from the log run, wearin' his spiked shoes. And up ahead there, he sees somethin' walkin' tall in the moon. He think it's a man and he wave. He git closer and see it's a bear, a-walkin' on his hind legs in the moonlight.

"Jimmy! Watch 'er!"

He don't hear me. He slam right inter that bear wi' his fist, a-cursin'. *Git outa me way, ye son of a whore.* The bear grab him. Jimmy kick the bear wi' his steel shoes.

"Watch out, old bear. That lad's rough!"

Bear don't hear. Jimmy kick like a mule, that boy, kick that bear agin and agin. The bear howlin' make yer hair stand straight up. The bear falls an' Jimmy land on his head, kickin' with them big spikes. The bear lay down, his tongue hangin' out.

"Ye killed him, Jim."

Jim don't hear. His arm's tore off. It's there in the bear's claws. Jim walk off, down the road, a-groanin' an' cursin'.

© © ©

PRIVATE RAZAMOV SPENT the long winter in his tent, drunk some of the time, mad occasionally, always bitter. The winds howled through his flimsy quarters, and he was forced to spend the day buried in his bunk, deep in blankets and pine boughs, cursing his Sovereign. The flower was a piece of dried stem fallen over, which he yet protected, constructing around it a small wooden case, made of pine twigs which he'd woven together, when his fingers were not altogether numb.

He had one visit from his court lady, the Countess, at Christmas. She brought a glowing feast, though declared at the climax of her visit that it was too cold to enjoy the delicate holiday pie. She seemed distracted, withdrawn, and he surmised, correctly, that she'd found other play at court. Her coolness did not touch him, nor was he troubled by the prospect of seeing her no more. The winter had matured his spirit, shattering all his ideas about the glory of a career, or the faithfulness of anyone. So when she said, "I won't be able to come again for a long while. I am going away, you see," he did not taste the sorrow of separation, but laughed, thus insuring that he would see her again, but not until springtime.

Bearlike, he curled in his bunk, escaping the cold in light, disagreeable slumber. He saw the scheme by which men grow mad—an allurement of complex curses and concern with the baffling. One night he certainly heard the voice of the Devil discoursing at great length in subtleties which contained the seed of insanity. Razamov was frightened, for he found he could not stop the voice. It delighted in his fear. When he ran out of the tent and stood beneath the stars, it took shape in the heavens.

Desperately, he straightened his uniform, polished his sword and, making himself in every way presentable to a monarch, took a position like that of an iron pole beside the dried flower. As he had been trained to, he banished thought, keeping constant attention, considering every sound, even of his own mind, as the possible movement of the enemy. The wind howled, a devilish shrieking.

He retired at midnight, rose himself for the watches at three-hour intervals through the night. By day he marched, beating a path around the field, enclosing his tent in a circle. The military tactics he had learned in his early training had been preserved in some secret cache of his brain, and while he marched, the formal movements of war flourished in his mind's eye, so that his spirit soared in abstract battle over the white sleeping field.

His Captain, on next visit, was met by a fierce, immaculate soldier, with eyes as clear as the winter sky, but at times seeming to be far off, in some extremity of reflection, though when spoken to, actually quite near, yes, right there, sitting at the table, joking again with the men.

There was good brandy to warm their bodies and lighten their hearts. Tobacco, too, for their long pipes, was opened, and they smoked and joked, and Razamov's laughter was quieter, like that of an old trooper. The Captain was aware of a change in his guardsman. Later, when the men had begun a game of cards, he and Razamov dropped out early. Standing together outside the tent, the Captain found himself ill-at-ease with his private, for he'd been prepared for the young man's entreaties to leave the post. Razamov, *au contraire,* seemed the very devil of a fellow—smooth as a shaving glass.

They walked along the beat Razamov had made around the field. As they walked, the Captain realized that in the time of peace that had befallen his army, they'd all grown soft, but for this one, the flower guard. When they had circled the field once full round, the Captain said, "Your promotion has come through," inventing that piece of business, but what was the difference if the orders were signed now or later? Razamov held the rank by decree of his own spirit.

"Thank you, sir," said the new Corporal.

"A raise in pay, of course," said the Captain.

"Would you keep it for me, sir?"

"Absolutely."

On parting, there were salutes, last encourage-
ments, and the soft tread of the horses through the
snow, slowly at first, upon the path made by Razamov
and, when they left it, they broke into a gallop, their
legs deep and the snow flying from their hooves.

chapter 7

A MUSICIAN in black overcoat which swept the side-walk entered the Golden Cafeteria. He wore white socks and sandals, which appeared now and then as if out of a robe. His head was bald except for two long streams of hair over each ear. His arms moved in long straight sweeps before him, exaggerated, like a soldier in a South American army. Of the mannerism, he seemed totally unconscious. Reading a piece of sheet music, he passed through the turnstile. The bong caused a noticeable twitch in his body, which responded completely to the note, seeming to rise off the floor.

Humming a passage from the sheet of music, he

selected a tray and got on line at the long counter. He
ordered yoghurt, homemade each morning by the
Golden kitchen, and a bowl of chicken soup. While
waiting for the soup to be spooned into the bowl, he
continued his humming, absorbed entirely in the musical progression on the sheet before him, but when a
distant *bong* came again from the turnstile, he ac-
knowledged it with a little leap.

Taking the soup then, and placing it on his tray,
he raised the tray. At once his arms became still, rigid,
in fact, holding the tray perfectly flat and steady in
front of him. The surface of the soup hardly rippled as
he left the counter and sought a table.

He found an empty table, set his yoghurt and
soup bowl down, then smashed one hand against the
empty tray, sounding it like a cymbal. Immediately a
busboy took it from his hands. He sat then, and
opened his package of crackers. Crushing them in a
single crunch of his right hand, he dropped the lump
of crumbs into the soup, and banged the soup spoon,
three times, on his head, which he shook with a maes-
tro's haughtiness, born of secret knowledge. He thrust
his spoon into the soup. The heat of the liquid, once in
his body, warmed him to such a degree that he removed from around his neck the sweater which he had
tied there as a scarf, hurling it tempestuously to the
floor, with the flourish of the podium.

Finishing his soup, he opened his briefcase, which
was stuffed to bursting. A sock hung over the edge, and
a broken pocket watch on a string. Sheet music was everywhere, and it was one of these sheets the musician
removed from the bag. He looked at it and laughed
contemptuously, then his mood changed drastically,

and he brought his face closer to it, his brows wrinkled with doubt, confronting it with a menacing gaze, like a ferocious dog which has spotted an intruder of formidable size. Slowly his frown relaxed. His fingers began fluttering, like tiny wings beating the air about the table, and he smiled, childlike. His hair, wild at the temples, seemed to rise electrically, producing a fuzzy halo about his mostly bald head. His sock-sandaled feet both went up and down, so that his chair soon began to rattle. A strange guttural noise escaped his mouth, dark and droning.

An old lady turned around in her chair to give him a withering look. Sensing her, he raised his eyes from the sheet of music and pointing one finger at her, cocked his thumb, firing a sweet beautiful high note at her, from his throat, so high it would seem the woman herself had sung it and that she was a grand diva. It was so right, so alarmingly clear, she lowered her eyes, as did the musician, returning to the score, tapping his feet with more vigor, so that the table began to rock.

◎　◎　◎

RAKER ENTERED the Rubens gallery. The room was filled with great work, and Raker seated himself in front of the largest canvas, a hunting scene. Despite the brilliance of the colors, it seemed ordinary: a lady of refinement on horseback, with her escort, a nobleman in grand hat, astride his own powerful steed. The lady's expression was coy, her body seated just so, and the gentleman was almost bowing to her, as if in a dance. Raker's eyes descended, to the horizon of the painting, beneath the horse's legs, where the dogs were tearing at the fox, and his heart leapt.

The fox was fighting savagely, teeth bared, fur bristling, the dogs upon him. Raker's gaze traveled further into the darkness, in the shadow beneath the horse's belly, and there he saw the Dog of Dogs, the Hound of Hell, head shaped like a helmet, eyes a cunning red, coming upon the fox. It was the true center of the painting, the dark, forbidding middle of the action of death. Raker felt himself white all over his body, as if in a faint, but he refused to move his eyes from the painting. Slowly he backed up and seated himself on a wood bench, still gazing at the highborn lady above, her face like paste, and the trapped fox below, snarling at the helmet-headed Hound of Hell which rose eternally from the center.

Raker nervously adjusted his feet, tapping them back and forth together, trying to rid himself of the sudden tightness that had entered his chest. Not feeling well. He tried to move, but it pained him. The painting had him in its grip, as if he were the fox. It must be gas, yes, a touch of indigestion from a Central Park hot dog. He tried to belch, but seemed to have no control over his chest or stomach. He wiggled his behind, trying to break wind. A bubble of pressure moved and grew within him. Just be calm, it will pass. He returned his gaze to the painting, continuing his investigation. Suddenly the features of the dog and fox dissolved.

The center, where the hound's head had been, was a vortex, seeming to shine in one moment and grow muddy the next, swirling and turning, sucking inward. Raker felt himself drawn into it. A terrible joy crossed his chest, and he experienced a loss of breath, as the winds of his system were inhaled from out of him by the wide, flaming nostrils of the Hound. Raker gasped. His illumination dawned. The painting was a dance, a field of radiance, with budding flowers of color opening everywhere on its surface, the entire canvas one great blossom with infinite shades and dimensions reflected in all directions and ever inward. In the wheeling rush of a thousand prisms was the world and Rubens.

Raker regained his breath with relief, but it left him again, and in the emptiness of his anxiety, he felt himself widening, deepening, going beyond man, out of reach of ancient cultures and crafts, as the world, with all its living mystery, retreated from him.

Shot with fear, Raker saw evil beauty laughing. The woman above on horseback knew nothing, nor did the man. They did not know that below them the trapped fox was Julius Raker. *I must leave this room, get away.* He tried to rise, but had lost control of his body. It did not seem real or awake, was limp, had fainted.

A sweet smell filled the room, like the smell of a church, but without the staleness of smoke, more like a woman's scented gown. Raker, terrified, tried to call, to the guard, to his wife, his sons, but could not form the words, nor find his throat. His panic leapt. He knew, suddenly, he was dying. The realization convulsed him, mind and body. Intensely sorrowful, mad with grief, he sought to buy time, offering up fortune and promise, and saw there was no time left. In the ever-widening moment, illuminations gathered, hideous, beautiful, pulsing wildly. The universe was a peacock, exquisite-eyed and blue, and was gone. The world was an old woman who knew his beginning and his end. The earth was Rubens and, finally, it was the dogs.

He was in the colors now, sinking through their fire.

Today is the day, after all. I have always known it, though it comes early, always too early. He heard the hunting horn, hollow, sounding the world, and the fire and the horn were one. He turned in the fire, saw an old man on the bench, slumped over, as if asleep. *Goodbye,* he called, from the depths of the flaming color wheel, which spun him, turning him to the left and down, then around and up.

The horn shattered the museum. Everything broke apart, the colors evaporating. Raker was an untouched canvas, white, primal, shining.

© © ©

"SURRENDER? NEVER!"

The exultant cry of Lord Beaverboard echoed through the underground corridor. He appeared to Hermit Perky in a uniform bemedaled. "King Leopold has surrendered the Belgian Army to the Gestapo."

"'ave some chips, Lord B," said Douglas Perky, filling a plate with potatoes he had just fried on his underground stove.

Lord Beaverboard nibbled a few. "This may be our last meeting, Perky."

"'ow's that, yer Worship?" Perky poured out two glasses of white wine.

"I am joining Queen Victoria's Rifles at the front. That is, what remains of them. We've suffered a severe setback, my dear fellow."

"Some vinegar for those, Lord B?"

"Thank you, yes. Of course, you will carry on here beneath the ground. Frankly, I see you as something of a symbol, living here, at home in England, in the safeness of your cave." Lord Beaverboard stood. "I expect it will be some time before we meet again." Lord Beaverboard touched the rim of his cap and left the cavern, for Dunkirk and a go at the Gestapo.

With his last charge of dynamite, the ornamental hermit knocked down a telephone pole on the roadway outside the Beaverboard estate, beneath which he was tunneling.

The army, fearing invasion by German paratroopers, sent a squad of soldiers in an armored van to investigate. The hollow roadway collapsed beneath the weight of the van and, as it sank out of sight, a newly promoted subaltern, Lieutenant Rodney Bushmaster Crumb opened fire with the machine gun mounted on the roof of the van, wounding himself and killing the mailman who'd just delivered the Beaverboard correspondence for the day. Lieutenant Crumb, son of Bushmaster Crumb, Member of Parliament, received the Distinguished Conduct Medal. The van was abandoned as a total wreck, and its bulletproof shell became the egress of the hermit's East wing. Often at night he sat in the submerged vehicle, aiming the machine gun at the sky.

"Oh, Mr. Perky!"

The hermit heard a strange female voice, far off, somewhere down the hallway of his catacomb. He waited.

"Mr. Perky, yoohoo!" The voice came nearer. The hallway echoed with female footsteps, hurrying, clicking. Then she appeared in the doorway of the central room, fat as a whale.

"I hope I'm not disturbing your contemplations," she said, briskly entering, indicating she did not care if Aristotle was on the brink of revelation. She wore a uniform with braids and badges. "I am Mrs. Bondyjig. I'll come straight to the point. We'd like to place a child in your hole. His father fell at Dunkirk, his mother is incapacitated."

"Mrs. Bondy, shall we retire into the den?" Perky led the way to the sitting room. Mrs. Bondyjig followed, enormous, like an operatic movement. Her hair was done in braids beneath her peaked military hat. She sat on the plush velvet couch.

"You have the room. Lady Beaverboard told me she would provide a bed and bureau for the lad. We shall bring him over tomorrow, if that's all right with you."

"Mrs. Bondy." Perky advanced toward the great woman.

"Yes, Mr. Perky?"

He moved like a storm trooper, reaching directly out to Mrs. Bondyjig's bosom, fondling it with deliberate squeezes. The astonished woman did not react for a moment, perhaps because of the superfluity of her flesh. By the time the shock had reached her brain, Perky was handling both her breasts with familiarity.

"My dear sir," she said, drawing herself to attention.

Perky did not retire. Quickly he opened the three main buttons of her uniform.

"Desist!"

Perky flung open her military tunic. Her flesh came into view, two gigantic globes of white, tucked against each other, encased in a colossal brassiere.

"Mr. Perky," said the outraged Mrs. Bondyjig, "I have fifteen foundlings to place this evening."

Perky continued fondling, removing her tunic completely, tossing it on the sofa. He was behind her then, working the fastener of her great harness. "This will only take a minute," he said, and the harness popped open. Quickly then, he encircled her with his arms, cupping enough of her bare breasts to make the middle-aged lady repeat herself with a tremble, "Mr. Perky, please." Then, as he continued to squeeze them, localizing his effort by tweeking her handsome nipples which bobbed like huge corks on the milky ocean, she said, "There's a war on."

Perky pressed himself against the tank of her backside. Rapidly for a hermit, he unzipped her skirt down the side. It fell to the floor, revealing her in her stays. Her skirt at her ankles, her breasts hanging bare, Mrs. Bondyjig stood in silence. Then, thinking desperately, she said, "Hitler is advancing."

Perky unhooked the buckles of her corset.

"The French have surrendered," sighed Mrs. Bondyjig, as her corset fell away, tugged over mammoth thighs, down past elephantine knees, falling finally atop her skirt around her ankles at the floor. "Step out of that, Mrs. Bondy, so you don't 'ave a bad fall," said the hermit, taking her hand.

"Mr. Perky, this is most irregular," said Mrs. Bondyjig, her great boomers swinging as she stepped from her piled clothing. Her last piece of underwear

was a pair of khaki panties with the Crown sewn upon
them. Perky worked deftly, inserting his ornamental
finger into the elastic and working it downward.

Mrs. Bondyjig stared at the Cézanne still life
which hung on the wall, given to the hermit by Lord
Beaverboard from his own collection. It was rich fruit
on the edge of a table, falling from a basket half-cov-
ered with linen. She remembered, a night long ago—
ages, it seemed, ago. The hermit traveled with her
panties down past the still-black muff of her grand
femininity, the triangular puff of light and shadows
through which Perky trailed his fingers, as the panties
went down, off her thighs, past her knees, to the floor.

Mrs. Bondyjig stood naked, magnificent in the
half-light of the cave, like a minotaur, lost.

"I'll just be a moment, Mrs. Bondy," said Perky.
The hermit stripped himself, while his guest remained
at attention, knowing it was foolish to try to cover her
large parcel of humanity. Then she felt the hermit's
scrawny naked body pressed against her own, insinuat-
ing itself into her many folds.

Their separate fleshes met, lonely, beneath the
wartime country. Perky embraced her head-on, burying his face in her great soft globes, like a man inside a
pudding.

Mrs. Bondyjig could remain at attention no
longer. Her knees went at ease. She felt herself sinking
to the rug. "Dunkirk," she said, vanquished. Long ago,
when I was a size ten, the late Mr. Bondyjig took me
boating, in the sunshine.

Perky climbed atop her, like a member of the Al-
pine Club taking the Queen of Mountains, the great
Himalaya. She spread out beneath him in all direc-

tions. There were two round native huts and low-lying vegetation. He searched for a handhold on the upward slope. The massive fleshes of her thighs came together on his hand, pressing it tightly.

"Mr. Perky, I implore you to release me."

Perky found the handhold he needed on the treacherous cliff. One of the best all-around men in England at the time, he lifted himself slowly into position by the solitary action of one arm only, until he was able to demonstrate to her the use of his more substantial climbing tool, the ornamental organ, which he slipped into her dark crevice with perfect accuracy.

"Mr. . . . Perky." It's been such a long time. I can still feel the rocking of the boat, the gentle rowing of the oar. She spread her legs apart, so Mr. Perky might have more room, then closed her thighs around him so he could not escape.

Perky thrashed in the great cavern. It was endless, powerfully scented, dripping with jewels.

Mrs. Bondyjig encircled him with her arms. War makes the night exciting. She felt all the sea and airmen passing through her, she was London, felt them prowling the dark doorway of a pub, going in, going out, covered with red kisses.

The ornamental hermit traveled through the bush, with rich thrills in his perky.

Mrs. Bondyjig understood the war effort more clearly now. The placing of the children must be taken care of, and each night, without fail, she must cheer the warriors. She could play the piano a bit. Her maid would make lovely things to eat. A sailor was eating a tongue sandwich. A tray of pickles, sweet and sour, was at the center of the table. All over her body egg salad was spread. Oh, the incessant knocking, Mr. Perky, please. Here we have a plate of fruit, soft-seeded melon, and a dish of nuts.

Perky tried to work his hands under the huge buttocks of Mrs. Bondyjig and he was partly successful, but he could not lift her. Still, he was able to load an exotic banana plant into the hold of the old troopship. With his other hand he steered her boomer, round and round, turning the ship sharply in the strange waters. For a moment, he thought he'd fallen out a window.

"*Mr. Perky,*" whispered Mrs. Bondyjig, giffy with stiffing, a shaken cloth, light as linen, blown in the wind, just a wisp of a girl in the meadow. The troops went over the side of her and down, hanging by guide ropes, carrying their death-dealing machines. Then the sky was filled with globes of light. Were they bombs or worlds?

Mrs. Bondyjig lifted her hips. A torpedo hit the ship without warning. It was several moments before the flames reached the Captain's bridge, where she was laying with that officer, playing with his whiskers and listening to tales of the China Sea. She trembled, as the sextant fell to the floor. A flame cracked her hold. Hoses were abundant. Children were being placed, nice little Perkies, a million strong. She cracked in half. The Captain confronted her, his organ of command still in the air, but his cap on correctly. She wailed over the ocean water, going down. Foam churned at the mortal wound in her, the delicious specter of death enveloping them all, that Sunday afternoon long ago in the boat with the late Mr. Bondyjig and the Allied Forces.

© © ©

PROFESSOR MONTROSE PUT THE KEY into his apartment door. It was a cellar dwelling, next to the town bowling alley. The sound of falling tenpins filled the air. He opened the door and pointed the way down the stairs for her. The staircase was lit by a small naked bulb. She went down before him in her trench coat and beret. Paris, he thought, cafés. Upon the wall was a large charcoal sketch of Santa Claus in a sled mounted with machine guns and pulled by reindeer marked with the insignia of the Nazi SS.

"It was here when I moved in," said Montrose.

He opened the door to the living room. Though it was daylight outside, the interior of the room was dim. He reached inside the shade of a hanging lamp and switched on a light bulb. The shade around it was made of a paper bag, which still had the grocer's penciled total on its side.

Upon one wall of the room was a mural, done in bright reds and greens, a tropical scene with strange birds and many naked, big-breasted women. Across the top was written *Thalassa Aloha.*

"Where Dutch sailors go when they die," said Montrose. "This place belonged to a peculiar little Dutch fellow, famous for his drunken parties. You'll notice over here a bullet hole in the wall. They threw him out at the end of June. That's when I took over."

She sat down on one of two low couches, set at right angles, with a small square table at the center of their union.

"Be careful you don't get stuck with a spring," said Montrose. "That couch appears to have been chopped in half."

Two small windows graced the living room. One, at sidewalk level, allowed a small portion of light inside. The other opened out beneath a dark porch.

"How about a can of beer?" Montrose went to the kitchen. The sound of the bowling alley grew louder; the kitchen looked directly out to the entrance of the sporting place. Montrose opened the refrigerator, found only one can of beer.

He dashed up the stairs, crossed the sidewalk, crawled over a wooden fence, dropping into the parking lot of the Cave. When he entered the bar, he was greeted by a Hungarian in black suit, playing the pinball machine with black gloves on.

"Did I ever tell you of my life in the sewer during the Revolution?" he asked Montrose. *"Get over there!"* He shook the pinball machine, giving it a savage jolt with his gloved hands.

"Easy there," said the bartender.

"A machine gun," said the Hungarian, "is a magnificent weapon, though useless against a tank."

"Two six-packs of Old Bohemian," said Montrose to the bartender.

She could be leaving the apartment right now, thought Montrose, as a dream flashed through his mind: He was taking curlers out of his hair, thousands of them. Friends were outside, waiting, blowing the horn impatiently.

"Here you go," said the bartender.

He left the Cave quickly, climbing back over the fence. I am suspended mid-air, attempting to reach my beloved. He looked down at the sidewalk window, trying to see into his apartment, but could only see across to the other wall and the painted women. Motion is impossible. Whatever distance we cover, first we must cover half that distance, and half the half, and half the half the half, inward, in infinite regression. I'm coming, Mother.

He grasped the knob. You, my God, are at the center of the paradox, unmoving, through eternity. He went quickly down the stairs. And you love women.

"Well," she said as he peered in, the two packs of beer in his arms, "that was fast."

"It's relative," he said, and went quickly to the kitchen, where he opened the cans and returned with them and two empty unmatching jelly glasses.

He was sitting on one couch, she on the other. Because of the lowness of the piece, her knees were raised, her dress, too, raincoat falling away, nylon knees and thighs, a thousand temptations in sheer veil. His stomach turned over. Dream: *Walking by a river, toward a bridge.*

Her eyes were big and dark, her eyebrows dark and heavy, shaped into rough crescents. Her nose was softly aquiline, her lips full, glazed with a transparent cosmetic. Through the window over her head came the sounds of the Cave—the ringing of the pinball machine, the sound of the jukebox:

You got to change your evil ways

"How long have you been at the University?" she asked, setting her glass on the table beside the open beer can.

He raised his own glass to his lips. The rich dark porter went down easily, and he drained the glass, pouring himself another. He wished she would remove her raincoat. "Let me take that raincoat." He reached forward, his hands aiming directly for her breast buttons.

She moved quickly, out of his reach and, standing, slowly unbuttoned her coat and removed it. With trench coats the material can bulge deceptively, but no, her breasts, as remembered, were appearing, through the cloth of her blouse, large, extraordinary.

"While you're up," said Montrose, "I'll give you the tour."

He showed her the kitchen, with another couch, ripped, battered, against the stone wall by the stove.

"I haven't done much decorating," he said. She was about five feet two or three, in short skirt. He could smell the perfume at her neck. He leaned his head forward to smell more of it. She walked away into the hall.

"The door to the bathroom is somewhat strange should you care to use it." He showed her how it slid along runners in the ceiling, where it jammed halfway, barely concealing the toilet and the obscene drawings on the wall. They turned the corner of the hall. He opened a door with windows in it. A dark damp smell came to them. "I don't go in there much. The Dutch fellow owned a rat. This was the rat's room. Of course, he had a cage, but still . . ." He closed the door.

"Where did he get the rat?"

"Sociology department. Quite tame, actually an idiot. They'd had him on a wheel, something to do with a study on the behavior of slum children."

"You're lying."

"The rat was bonkers. I met him when the Dutch fellow moved out. Nice little creature. Here's my so-called bedroom."

Montrose switched on the light to the small room. The walls were like those of the other room—grey stone. A bamboo screen hung down from the ceiling. Behind it, through its cracks, she saw a bed. Montrose went to the wall and pulled open a small metal door, the vent of a chimney. He brought out a bottle of wine. "I had to drive fifteen miles for this."

His desk was piled with papers, books, a freshly-laundered shirt, a small plastic skull, an empty beer bottle. Amidst the rubble was a prophylactic, exposed, except for a paper wrapper around its rolled middle. Montrose followed her eyes to the dusty contraceptive. Still, it is better than her coming upon, perhaps, filthy undershorts on our first day. Where are they? Yes, under the bed, peeking. He gave them a kick into the shadows, recalling his mother's words about keeping his feet clean, lest he be struck by a bus and, as the crowd gathers around his body, from which the shoes have been tossed off by the impact, socks dragged to shreds along the pavement, it is seen that he has dirty feet.

"It isn't very mathematical, I'll admit," he said, waving a hand over the desk, willing it to rearrange itself neatly.

She lowered her eyes, seemed to be lost in thought, not about him.

"Well, shall we have a drop of this? And some lunch?" He held the bottle to the light.

"I must be going," she said.

"Because my room is a pigsty? Please," said Montrose. "My feet are clean."

"I beg your pardon."

Once he'd had an evening, when he was a student, with a lady history professor, married. They stopped at a roadhouse, ate supper, and he took her home. Only years later, suddenly waking, like a man who has been held in hypnosis, did he realize that she had wanted him to make love to her.

"I have no pretence," he said, indicating with a sweep of his hand the wreckage of his rooms. "I am a natural man."

He went to the living room, poured wine into his jelly glass, on top of the remnants of beer foam. She appeared in the doorway, her face in shadows.

Montrose concentrated on her vagina, envisioning its tangles of fire, downward turning, into a little pointed goat's beard. If seen from behind, curls would be hanging down, in faint appearance between her round cheeks. I must register my new students today.

He jumped up, went to her. She ran for her trench coat. He'd hung it over a kitchen chair, was there before her, knocking over with his hand a box of macaroni which was on the table. "Stay for lunch," he said, picking up the box. He ran his eyes over the instructions. *Do not blanch,* he read. "Do you know what that means?"

"It means don't run cold water over them."

He embraced her. Breasts, round belly, soft experience of woman.

His lips came toward her. She wanted to run, closed her eyes. Distant shouting merged with the thunder of tenpins as he kissed her, and she dreamt:

They walked along the Mall. She had so much work to do, was captive to a thread this young professor had wound around her. At any moment she could break away.

He said lunch. She felt light. Men always made her a stranger to herself. He seemed preoccupied, so was she. He was tall, with deep simian creases in his cheeks. Apelike, he fascinated her. She should be in the library, with Albert Einstein and Nicolas Bourbaki.

"I have a great love of streets," he said.

She was secure when calculating the relationship of rays dissecting each other in a circle. Here, with this strange man, she was beyond the protection of her circle, beyond Einstein and Bourbaki. She was a comet, wild, without course.

"It is exceeded only by my love of alleyways," he said, as they turned off the street into the shadows of a small court.

Stepping over to the back door of a movie theater, he waved her beside him. She heard, through the door of the theater the soundtrack of the film:

"Here's looking at you, kid."

Her hands were in her trench coat pockets, her slim briefcase held to her waist by the pressure of her elbow. She stepped alongside him, looking at the points of her shoes and the line of her ankles. He wanted to be with her for her ankles, her legs, silly, thrilling.

Outside the backdoor of a restaurant, she looked through the screen with him, into the noisy kitchen.

"Often," he said, "I stand here."

She looked from the distant stove up to his face, in profile, his large forehead, heavy brows, wide nose and heavy sloping chin, apelike, or juglike, for his head seemed like a large pitcher, not unattractive.

There was noise, men laughing, a crashing sound. "The bowling alley," he said, pointing her down a flight of steps into a damp cold embrace; a paper bag lit up; she sat, feeling her skirt rise up her thighs. The day has turned out altogether different.

He suddenly raced past her, hurtling up the stairs. She was alone. Now was the time for rational thought.

One entire wall of the room was covered with naked women and birds.

He came down the stairs and entered with two cans of beer.

"Here is my bedroom."

"I must be going."

The danger blossomed, rose quickly, a box of macaroni.

She was in his arms, kissed and opened, her nature rising up. She wetted his tongue with her own. Against her belly, she felt the warm irresistible—number one.

© © ©

REVEREND CUPPLEWAITE LIFTED another forkful of cake to his face, slipping the chocolate substance into his mouth. He smiled at Sally Fifer, and she smiled back. He raised his teacup, and she raised hers. Like a hot bath, the tea had lost the first heat and become less vivifying. And like the determined bather, bent on continuing delicious submersion, Reverend Cupplewaite raised the teapot, which had retained its hotness almost entirely, and added more hot to his own cup and to Sally's.

Their eyes met.

"Of course, Mother's fruit cake is also a family secret," said Sally, adjusting her skirts.

Reverend Cupplewaite put the newly hottened cup to his lips, and the steam fogged his glasses for a moment, casting Sally Fifer behind an opaque window. "I don't believe I've had your mother's fruit cake."

"Oh, you must have some!" exclaimed Sally, shocked at the Reverend's ignorance of the fruited joy. "It's so moist, dark or light. She puts cherries into it."

Reverend Cupplewaite went to the window, tilting it open a few more degrees. Putting one finger in his collar, he tried to loosen its stiffness. Out in the hills, at night, there is a woman said to perform with a black snake a religious rite.

Reverend Cupplewaite looked down at his plate again, where the painted coach and horses were beginning to appear once more, riding out of the chocolate. "And how is your father, my dear?"

"He's in the woods," said Sally.

"The life for a man," said Reverend Cupplewaite, absent-mindedly. What does she do with the snake, that is the question.

"He cut his finger badly," said Sally.

"Is that so?"

"Almost took it off completely."

"The logger sees many a danger." Reverend Cupplewaite removed another piece of cake. Out galloped the second horse, seemingly ready to rear.

"He's had several stitches in his head." Sally rose, moving her chair just a bit more forward, so that her voice might carry more naturally to Reverend Cupplewaite. There was the better part of a pot of tea left, and they always finished it together. "Yes," she went on, "a tree limb came down and cracked him."

© © ©

O THE JESUS BLEEDIN' TAY ROAD O

Wee fairies in the leaves, a-singin'. Their dancin', ain't it nice, though. Sometime the day shake me by the throat.

Fallin' through Tay Road no. Some folks goes along easy, never mindin' the eye in the sky, the fire in the head.

O the Jesus hell-fer-goin' Tay Road O
snakes
inside me. Momma dropped the dish and the pieces are still flyin', looky them goin' past the sink sa slow.

Little birds cheepin'. Wigglin' their tails. Sooner be you little bird than me. Climbin' up through the sky, every now and agin, walkin' on the clouds, queer thing fer a man ter be doin'. I ain't regular that way. I got a Jesus crack in me head and I come out there and go floatin' aroun'. Right out the top o' me head, inter the sky.

Stones is a-talkin'. *We the oldest men.* Fellers, I been

aroun' Tay Road ferever. I 'member back in the real old days I was a stone meself. Ye ain't done, boys, not by a long stroke.

Head hurt like a son of a whore. Momma, don't whip me no more. Trees is Jesus green right now. Seen a moose wi' her yearlin'. Standin' proud, don't ye know? Walked right acrosst the road slow. Some feller like ta plug her, not me, no. Ye shoot yerself ye shoot a moose. Looky them goin' there, sa nice. His legs is a little weak. I see 'em ever time I come ter this spot, they's a-crossin'.

Sometime I ain't nobody.

◎ ◎ ◎

SPRINGTIME CAME to the field some twelve miles from St. Petersburg, where Corporal Razamov protected the dead flower of Catherine. His first visit of the season was from the Countess, who was pregnant. She came to tell him that the child, if a boy, would be enlisted in the Preobrazhensky Regiment. If a girl, she would become a serving woman of the court, where she could amass, if clever, much money. In either case, steps of discretion had been taken by friendly figures to save mother and child from embarrassment.

"Of course, you are not to see the child, nor ask for it."

"Why, then, have you come?" Corporal Razamov lit his pipe, studying the face of the stranger with whom he had laughed in summer.

"I wanted you to know," she said.

The phrase remained with him after she had

gone, through the springtime, into summer. He repeated it over and over to himself, trying to extract from it some understanding of woman, until finally the words lost all meaning. And then he understood something of woman.

Catherine came in summer. Perhaps Corporal Razamov had sensed she would return after the cycle of the seasons. Or perhaps he saw no point in guarding a corpse, and so he had gone to the field and found a new flower of the same family as the old dried one, and made the substitution, constructing around the transplant a fence of wood, like a small stockade.

When the scarlet carriage, decked with gold and silver, appeared, Razamov was prepared. The Empress came across the field alone, slowly, wearing the uniform of his regiment, wearing it well, for she had natural dignity and the mind of a king. Razamov came to attention beside the flower. Seeing the colors of his regiment on the Empress, he recalled again her now legendary *coup d'état*, when she'd led the military to an uprising, marching from barracks to barracks in her long skirts, rallying the men in the overthrow of her husband.

Catherine was forty. Her court was the most splendid in the world. Her clothes, her palaces, her gifts to those in favor, were fabulous. As she crossed the field, she felt again the charm of a country girl's life. As a princess, she had never known such simple joy. Now, as Empress, she tasted it, though it was only a game, not blessed by natural abandon, for Voltaire and King Frederick were her correspondents, and affairs of international dimension continued to pass through her head. My, what a handsome soldier! Of course Captain Groot would pick the right man.

"Your Imperial Highness." Razamov saluted her, placing his sword at her disposal.

She stepped past him to the fence, looked down at the white flower. Though she acted as Head of the Orthodox Church, leading the elaborate ceremonies of St. Petersburg in pearl-laden vestments, bearing a jeweled cross, she was not religious. But now she knelt in wonder at a mystery. She had enemies within her country and without. She and the flower had survived another year of intrigue, flattery, and death. She and the flower . . . Voltaire would laugh and call her superstitious, like all her people. She would not write Voltaire of this.

She stood, looked up the gently sloping hillside, where Razamov's tent was pitched, on the summit, to escape the spring thaw. "Let me see your quarters, Corporal," said the Supreme Commander of the Army.

The tent was neatly kept, with table, chair, and bunk. The plain masculine simplicity appealed to Catherine's sense of order, which she never imposed on her own quarters, wild as an Eastern king's, her throne room like the fan of a peacock. She removed her hat, laying it on the writing table. Her hair was piled in cunning knots atop her head. Her face had lost the severe pointedness of her youth, was now softer and less strained.

The sides of the tent were bright with the spring sun. The Empress, naked on the narrow bunk, stroked the bare back of the soldier. In the field, the spring wind blew gently over the different flowers. At the scarlet coach, the old driver and a lone guard played at cards. Razamov sat on the edge of the bed, staring at the floor.

The horn of war sounded in Catherine. She met it with her flanks. Her husband had misused her; now he was dead, smothered beneath a mattress. She tossed upon the bunk, as empires moved within her. Mother of Russia's breasts were swelling now, to a soldier's touch. In the field, the late afternoon insects droned. Upon the coach, the old driver smiled, laying down a hand of queens.

Razamov lit the lamp. Catherine made him remain naked and herself refused to dress. She paraded before him. He smiled at the smooth white skin of her royal rump. Great Catherine groaned, clutching the sheets.

The field was in shadow. Fireflies appeared. The old driver and the lone soldier returned from a short walk down the road, enjoying the silence of the twilight hour.

"Is there anything else you would like?" The Empress lay on the bunk, enjoying her body's glow in the lamplight.

"Yes," said Razamov, seated on the edge of the table, "I should like something to read."

"I shall send you Voltaire," said Catherine. She might have made this soldier a captain, a general, a prince. For this insult, she stood and went toward the chair where her clothes were piled. Her breasts moved as she walked. Razamov placed his hands upon them again as she bent over her clothes. She sighed, closing her eyes, as war resumed, a fiercely barbarous outburst against the sovereign walls at the rear of her palace. She might, after all, make him lieutenant.

chapter 8

THE MUSICIAN of the Golden Cafeteria stood and tied the arms of his sweater around his neck, draping the front of it over his chest. He buttoned his enormous overcoat and, turning to the great floor-to-ceiling mirror, he contorted his nose, lips, and eyes into the features of a friendly demon. He then added remarkable pig and duck noises, soft and gentle.

Nearby, two women were dining. One, an attractive bleached blonde, wore a nurse's cap, on which was the insignia of the old-age home around the corner from the cafeteria. Her companion, with hair slightly streaked by grey, seemed more settled, less anxious than the nurse, who was talking with marked desperation.

"I've got to get married."

"Nobody has to get married," said the nurse's friend.

"I've got to get married," repeated the nurse. "I'd marry anyone." She looked around the cafeteria, her eyes traveling over one man after another—mailman, salad-man, truck driver, student. Her eyes stopped at the musician in sandaled socks, flying hair, overcoat to the floor, fingers rapping furious time on the side of his briefcase as he madly stuffed sheet music back inside and slammed it shut.

"I'd even marry him."

He turned toward them, eyes blazing. On the other side of the cafeteria the turnstile bonged. He lifted in the air.

"You wouldn't," said her friend.

"I would," said the nurse.

He picked up his briefcase and passed by them, his arms again swinging like a South American general, his entire body deep in melody and reverberation, hearing their conversation as part of a chorus against which his theme was woven, eternal, circling, supreme.

© © ©

JULIUS RAKER RESTED in the colorless canvas of infinite tranquillity. After many ages of rest had passed, delicate strokes of color began to fall upon the canvas. A sky of blue was born of an invisible brush, then trees, ground, grass. The painting was deep, living, and he found himself walking in it, along a stone path.

The landscape was magic, like the molecules of a

dream, and the dream had persistence. His painted garden grew peacefully, undisturbed by that fickleness dreams are plagued with, the constant shifting and dissolving of their elements. Raker walked in the paradisical garden, beyond the trauma of death.

A pool appeared in the ground, sparkling, with radiant fish in its waters. He walked to it and looking down, caught his reflection. His face was unmarred by the puffiness and weak bones of his past, though traces of that face remained, hidden beneath a new countenance which had built upon and improved the old.

He wore a simple white robe. His hands were folded at his chest in a prayerful posture. It cost him no effort to hold them that way and he walked on.

Through the trees, he caught sight of stone work, and happily went forward to the museum. He was met at the door by a familiar figure—the large-domed head, the long porcelain robe of the Chinese Sage from the glass case on the second floor. The Sage bowed and Raker returned the bow.

They entered the vast splendid storehouse. The works of art lived in their stillness. Raker sensed that he would grow wise here, with ages past and future at his disposal. Elated, his creativity sparked, flamed, casting brilliant light in the Great Hall of the museum.

"How lovely, how lovely!" said the Porcelain Sage. "You are on that plane called Universal Peacock."

Raker expanded his tail outward in myriad eyes of ravishing color, out and out of himself, elegant feathers of soft green-gold and purple, with blue ear-bells and black feather-lace crown. He remained that way through the first day, enjoying the vision of beauty that had sprung from himself. Matching the loveliness of his feather fan was a feeling of love—love hypnotic, warm and dreaming, love vital and fierce, strutting in the garden of the sun, love, a bird of paradise, love, the King of Birds, love, bells, beauty. He walked in the heat and sang, entranced through the afternoon in the sand, where his tiny feet made fine lines. The lines and feathers were so familiar—had he this dream somewhere, long ago?

"It is an ancient station," said the Porcelain Sage. "Many walk with you in this moment, many universal birds."

Later in the long day of song and reflection, another bird was noticed in the garden. In amongst the flowers was she, eyeing the fan of the Universe. He went to her, the King Bird, and they played. The Porcelain Sage turned toward the water, assuming his formal posture, hands in his drooping sleeves, in his own deep trance, until he blended into the garden, a silent detail.

So the birds were left alone, on the first evening of Paradise.

© © ©

LONDON WAS under siege. The ornamental hermitage had been coverted into a bomb shelter. It was deep, well made, and though it shook a bit when bombs fell close by, it did not surrender its walls. Hermit Perky now shared his underground home with several homeless families, and when the air raids came other nearby households flocked to his ditch. He turned all his rooms over to the invading neighbors, keeping only the submerged armored van for himself. Through Lord Beaverboard's influence, the hermit received fifty crates of ammunition for the machine gun mounted atop the van.

Occasionally Mrs. Bondyjig visited him, to place another underground child.

"Mr. Perky, we mustn't." Her dress uniform was pulled up over her head, revealing the twin flanks of her buffalo. She rocked her hips quietly, for there were children about.

"I 'ear bombers," said Perky, leaping off the great lady and scrambling up to his machine gun.

"Mr. Perky, my dear." Mrs. Bondyjig lifted herself after him, her bare cheeks whumping like a kettle drum. The hermit sat naked in the gun turret, except for his air warden's helmet, scanning the sky. Mrs. Bondyjig modestly toyed with his gun barrel. The bombers appeared, silver eagles caught in the searchlights of the city. Perky opened fire.

Rat-tat-tat-tat-tat-tat-tat-tat-tat-tat

The night was aflame. In the dark an umbrella store was burning. In Africa, Lord Beaverboard prepared his men to defend against mosquitoes. Mrs. Bondyjig, shaking from the thunder of the machine gun, gallantly clutched to that weapon she loved to fire, in the night, in the burning.

Rat-tat-tat-tat-tat-tat-tat-tat-tat-tat

The hermit pivoted in his gunner's seat, swinging the machine gun after a shining bomber, Mrs. Bondyjig clinging to his heated barrel. In the crossed threads of his scope he sighted the vulnerable underbelly of a *Luftwaffe* fighter pilot.

High in the night sky, the daring flyer rode handsomely. Below, the earth was incandescent with tracer bullets. He loved Gerta, the serving girl at the tavern, with her laughter and red kerchief, bending over the cooler.

Rat-tat-tat-tat-tat-tat-tat-tat-tat-tat

Sweeping low over the London suburbs the dashing airman came to the threaded crossroads of his destiny—shot to pieces by a naked hermit. The machine gun bullets ripped through his fuselage, surprising him beyond belief. The serving girl's red kerchief fluttered in the sky as he turned over in smoke and fire and slumped forward into her arms. The world was red!

"Bull's-eye, Mrs. Bondy!"

"Yes, darling, yes," sighed Mrs. Bondyjig, as the burning aircraft crashed in a distant field, and she fired a triumphant salvo of flesh-fire juices from the hermit's semiautomatic. It caught her in the eye, for it was an unusually powerful burst, the hermit being over-excited by the evening's sport.

◖ ◖ ◖

MONTROSE IN his mildewed cellar was master of the next move, of his hand now, to her breast then, lightly, upon the silk blouse, slowly closing on the truth. Over her shoulder he saw his frying pan on the stove, filled with grease.

She sighed, raising her breast to him. Her apartment was in order, she would return to it later, and nothing would be disturbed. He squeezed the softness, yes, they like it. She came from a coal town, in a house just off the highway, opening my blouse.

Inserting his fingers under her shoulder strap,

then down into the cup, Montrose came upon the bump-rough of her nipple, the periphery, and tried desperately to reach the genial protuberance itself, but was a nail's breadth short, held by the infernal bindery of her bra. There wasn't a moment to waste; they were plainly visible through the kitchen window to anyone who came into the parking lot on their hands and knees, as children often did, to mock him while he ate his meager lunch. He lifted and carried her into the hallway, past the rat's room, to his bedroom.

Her skirt up over her thighs, she kissed him on the neck, wishing she knew him better. Wrapping her arms around his neck, she licked his ear. He raised the bamboo shade, revealing his unmade bed.

The sheets seemed yellow. Is it a reflection from the bamboo? Her high heels dangled from her toes as he laid her on the bed.

He lit a candle mounted in the mouth of a beer bottle. The bottle was covered with wax, a dramatic thing left behind by the Dutch chap. The room flickered with shadows, as it had no window. He slipped into bed beside her, lowering the bamboo blind. The candle remained outside, glowing, its flame broken in the slatted bamboo. He crossed over her body, so he could rest on his left elbow and work with his right hand, the customary Hindu love prelude. He had increased the power of his gonads through *veerasana*, the Heroic Pose, which had the double blessing of producing, in times of leanness, such as he'd long endured, an acceptance of celibacy.

She felt it falling away, her blouse, the day. He touched her on the shoulders, and she felt her bra straps losing their tension, falling off onto her arms. He was over her then, with both hands, and carefully he pulled the cloth cups down, like a sheet from a sleeper, unveiling the two moons and the rising mountains of the moon. She looked at his ape-face, in their bamboo hut, in the jungle.

Montrose gazed at her breasts. A light brown circular patch was at the center of each, and in this patch was another circle of irregular little dotted bumps. Rising from the center of the circles were her nipples, turning over and in at the top, like the mouths of tiny volcanoes. Montrose, from the heights of sensuality, lifted her, to remove her blouse.

She toyed with his shirt, trying to open it. His chest—a dark, hairy ape. She squeezed his flat breasts, testing their hardness. Her hand went into his armpit, to the wet hairs.

Her skirt came open, and he slipped it down; it was spring, only panties covered her, along with the straps of her garter belt, a black and red frilly. He pulled the skirt over her knees, which she bent, kicking her legs, sending it off, over her toes, to the foot of the bed with the other clothes. Her stomach was white, round, descending into black panties. Then the white of her thighs took over, until the grey tops of her stockings began, making her legs shine, down to her toes, wiggling, elusive patterns of jewels and caravans, purple, gold, laced black, like an eyelash fluttering, yet fleshy, true human, perspiring, and when she raised her arms over his neck, he saw the shadow in her armpits, where she had shaved.

She toyed with his belt buckle, lazily, and touched his hard, flat stomach. Far off, she heard the crash of the bowling alley, as he unbuckled her garters and removed her stockings, caressing her thighs, gently coming closer, running his finger along the elastic, inside the edge, touching her, going through the curls, touching her. Ecstasy. It was so sad, all her lovers gathered there. He enjoys touching it. My legs are bare. She spread them, touching her toes to bamboo and stone.

He pulled the black panties down, returned his hand. She closed her eyes and let him separate the lips. Wet. He's there now, no stopping, so sensitive, so into the lips, the place of passion sunning, fingering my— one finger, two fingers—this, this fingering my delicate lips fingering. She whispered, touching at his pants. Then they were gone and in the shadows, caught by the flickering candlelight in the jungle hut, the snake danced. She reached out and touched it, with one finger on the eye. A tiny white tear came out, love sad, white love; she wiped it on her thigh and brought her hand back again, closing her fingers around it, ecstasy, feeling it hard in her hand. Now they were lovers, now she could tell him, what secrets, what daydreams, but she would not, after all, tell him anything.

She raised her legs, leading him, lingering the snake's head at her lips for a moment, nuzzling it there, letting it taste just the slightest softness of the hood, just the first wet edges, slipping it just a little bit in, covering the snake's head with it now, feeling the shape of it in the labias, a snake's heart in the mouth of time, and then she raised herself to it, and it went slowly in and down, his ray into my center, into me, into me, until she was pressed tight against him and it was all the way in. She tested it here and there, moving herself on it, new and wonderful man, can he know how I feel with him stuck up in me there so good I feel with him up in me there?

He rose above the afternoon with her, searching the red sky for knowledge, extreme in carnality, containing the riddle of consciousness, why it came forth. He heard moaning, worlds below, saw her face beneath him, eyes closed, felt her breasts, her stomach, her thighs, and the touch of her ankles.

She solved without paper several elaborate ideas. They were two spheres of different radius, he-she, and though different, had structural coherence. Ecstasy. His prick perpendicular to the right angle of my legs. She saw that in the higher dimensions the perpendicular rays were intertwined, and there was more to be said.

Montrose floated his own dream, in the flaming tent of her special counsel, where he learned volumes. She wrapped her ankles around his, so they were tighter together, wound like infinities. His flesh was continual surprise to hers. Bamboo. Damp sheets. You. He kept tilting her upward, so that it went down in further, into the hidden center. They would stay like this in the jungle, entangled ecstasy bamboo. She undulated against him.

Montrose matched his motion to hers. The hairs of their consorting tangled, parted, tangled again. His gonads were swelling, preparing their emissary. After much thought and experimentation, she had designed the perfect organ, long ago—the purse of fire, ever new in young girls, to trap him, and keep him spinning. He was powerless before its red desire.

She raised her ankles higher, winding them behind his calves to satisfy herself, pushing against the centerpole of the stars, bending it back inside her, so that it threatened her belly. She shook upon it, then bent it back again, and it catapulted her through rays of sensation. She struck her own center and came in African earrings of great length. They stood over the water talking. *You see now?* said Einstein. *Yes,* she said, *I see.* She unwound her ankles and spread her legs into a terrific V, as he pounded her and she winked her coming on his penis, ringing it with that most sophisticated kiss.

Her orgasm passed through Montrose, beaming into his balls and brain, all is OK with the world. He saw himself in the mirror of her release, and he was riding in a beautifully curtained basket, carried by an elephant. By God, he was handsome, with his mandrill's face of bright color, a prince of the philosophic treasure. His hands moved, in delicate gesture, making the symbols of fascination. I love you, in the cellar of my existence, in the tower of my fancy. Here I go, here I go.

In the flower-factory of his gonads, trained to yogic heroics, the stream of shining surrender was born. It leapt from Lord Shiva's mountain-rock and coursed along the winding trail. A god's reflex, it began as delight and became ever more sweet as it rose, up, up, original essence from the ancestral ocean.

◎ ◎ ◎

"AND WHAT OF our poor Mrs. Lemming passing away?" asked Sally, taking the Reverend's plate and adding another slice to it, burying again the horse and carriage.

"Yes, a pity," said Reverend Cupplewaite. "Still, she was an old person."

"We think we'll never grow old," said Sally, cutting herself a piece of cake.

"That is so," said Reverend Cupplewaite.

"But time catches up." Sally licked a drop of chocolate icing from her fingertip.

"Oh, well," said Reverend Cupplewaite.

They sat in silence, as the flies flew and marched in the sunlight. Reverend Cupplewaite closed his eyes again. Except for the flies, Tay Valley was quiet. Sally Fifer hummed softly, so quietly her voice seemed not part of the room, but a memory of someone singing. She had a lovely little voice, unknown to anyone.

Reverend Cupplewaite felt himself slipping off again, as undersea voices rose up, calling. He spun briefly, in a whirlpool, saw a girl with shells in her hair. Waking, he raised his head, turning to Sally, who quickly ceased her humming. For a moment, he did not recognize her; she seemed uncommonly pretty. Then slowly his mind returned, and he saw it was mere Sally Fifer, with a plate of cake. He smiled, as at an old dog, and turned back to the window. The blazing angle of the sun had changed, the window was now cooler.

"Your garden is grand this year," said Sally, rising and walking to the window. The edge of her skirt brushed the arm of his chair, rustling for a moment over his little finger.

© © ©

O THE TAY ROAD O

Field flowers laughin'. Million birds in front o' the sun. Am I home in me bed, a-dreamin' fer sixty year? Yer too much fer me, Lord. I cain't stand yer bleedin' face o' birds and wings, the sky all a-flutterin'.

Sometimes is worse than others, this is worse. Steppin' through the flamin' dust. Mouths everywhere, ter swallow me. Some fear death, not me. I been dead fer years. Dead 'er dreamin'.

Yer trees is prayin' to ye, Lord. They ain't cursed wi' feet. Some folks fear the dark. Not me. I am the dark.

Horse comin' out o' the sun, fire and sparks. *Momma.*

Yes, Herman. She come outa the earth, her eyes closed, ter proteck me.

Momma, I'm blowed ter smithereens.

Don't cry, Herman. We walk back inter me bedroom. She lights a candle.

Momma, I got two heads, see the lightin' jump from one ter the other.

Don't cry, Herman. It's into bed with you now.

O, what a bad dream. Got ta be a way out o' here. Don't see it. O, what a Jesus bad dream!

© © ©

IN THE FALL, Corporal Razamov received by special courier a small scroll, tied with a pink ribbon. It contained words from the Empress of the most intimate nature; also, the promise of a promotion, and a jewel, worth, she said, 150,000 rubles, by which she hoped he would remember her.

Shortly thereafter, Corporal Razamov received his first leave. A formal changing of the guard was made, and Razamov showed his replacement the supply hut, the powder magazine, the stream. He then packed his razor and brush and rode off on the horse which had been brought for him.

The horse, sensing its rider's mood, showed its speed, and the autumn leaves danced beneath the flashing hooves. After their first exaltation, Razamov reined in the mount and relaxed in the saddle, his sword flopping gently against the slowly rocking flank of the beast.

St. Petersburg frightened him. The buildings, the citizens, the movement loud and chaotic, all produced a dizziness in him, as if he were caught in a whirlwind. Many soldiers walked the street in the different regimental colors.

Razamov, drunk, marched happily by night with comrades, singing the old songs. Men, men, the company of men, brave, reckless, love of the wars. One of his company, a tall swaggering Lieutenant, talked to the innkeeper. To see the Lieutenant standing there, the lines of his uniform, the shine of his boots, the careless way he spoke, was for Razamov a testament, indeed, a sacrament; he drank the sight in and glowed with warmth. Here were men sure of themselves, like eagles, not flowers, eyes fierce and free. His great solitude made him susceptible now to every trace of movement, to every inflection in the coarse, grand voices of the men; they dubbed him Corporal Ghost, for he seemed to them like a man returned from the dead, with his wide, staring eyes and his soft, timorous voice.

"Corporal Ghost would like more wine, thieving

landlord!" cried the Lieutenant, tossing coins at the eager, happy proprietor.

"Yes, gentlemen," said the landlord, "he shall have whatever he wishes. The young man on leave should not be deprived of the pleasures of the vine."

"Shut up," said the Lieutenant, "and bring the wine before I kill you."

"Gentlemen, please, remove your elbows from the table but a moment while I set down these several choice bottles from the cellar. Not everyone drinks from these."

"Yes, only the drunkest of us, who don't know the difference any longer. This swill was his wife's bath water, gentlemen. We drink her greases, which make us braver than David!"

Razamov studied each face as if it were a sacred tablet. He saw men's souls this night. From childhood to the grave, their looks told all—eyes, mustaches, voices, smiles, lives, life, love! He stood, called out a toast to love.

"Yes, love!" echoed the Lieutenant. "Corporal Ghost must have love before this night is out. Well, we know where to find it, eh?"

"Yes, but stay awhile like this," said Razamov. "We mustn't rush."

"No, by God, we mustn't," said the Lieutenant. "The man who cannot take his pleasure slowly is a barbarian."

Their number grew, several more tables were filled and drawn up to theirs, and the landlord bolted the door. "A private party, now, gentlemen. I know you prefer it that way."

Razamov went through the dark corridor to the

back yard of the place. The night, laughter, music of stringed instruments were his soul. I have been sleeping in the field and have just wakened. He stumbled back through the corridor.

"I am starved!" he cried, returning to the room. "Listen, I tell you, I am dying of hunger and thirst."

"Corporal Ghost is regaining his color," said the Lieutenant. "He needs some red meat. Innkeep, come let me tear off your ears."

"Yes, honored guest?"

"First, bring us food, from wherever your mad wife has hidden it. Then more of this foul wine, and finally . . ." The Lieutenant put his arm affectionately around the innkeeper's shoulders ". . . and finally, take this." He handed the keeper a pile of rubles. "Wrap it in a note, signed with my name, and deliver it to . . ." He named the young lady.

"Immediately," said the innkeeper.

"I have returned from the grave," said Razamov, sitting down at the table.

chapter 9

I<small>N SPRINGTIME</small>, the Golden Cafeteria places a number of fruit pies in its window. The crusts are high and flaky, stuffed with apples, berries, peaches.

Two men sat by the window on Sunday morning, reading the *New York Times* and the *Daily News*. They ate their breakfast, not speaking, until one of them, older, grey-haired, wearing heavy horn-rimmed glasses, said, "*Blondie and Dagwood* is archetypal."

The other one, a younger man, did not look up from the *Times* nor acknowledge in any way his companion's remark.

"My father," said the older man, "slept on the couch, facing in, exactly as Dagwood does. Mother, of

130

course, was not so clever as Blondie." He laid down the comic strip and rattled the other man's paper. "Damnit, you're not listening to a word I'm saying."

"No, Donald," said the other man, continuing to read *The Week In Review.*

"There is something vegetable about you on Sunday mornings," said the grey-haired man. He put the paper down and picked up his toast. "How can you sit there reading that disgusting intellectual rag, while I am speaking of my childhood?"

"Yes, Donald," said the younger man, turning to the world roundup of editorials.

"Excuse me," said the older man, "I'm going to the men's room."

◎ ◎ ◎

JULIUS RAKER AND THE PORCELAIN SAGE walked in the garden of the museum. Maidens of marble graced the grounds, moving in slow dance, a stone dance, with gestures that formed in infinite slowness. At first glance, they seemed quiet and still, but if watched closely the graceful slowness of their movement became apparent. "At night," said the Sage, "when the grounds are completely still, one hears the music to which they move. It is the roaring of dragons."

A crane flew over the lake, calling against the sun, and Raker suddenly remembered a dirt road upon which he'd walked, pulling a wagon. "I have lived before," he said.

"Indeed," said the Sage.

"I . . . was mad," said Raker, as the memory asserted itself, grey, fragmented. *O the Tay Road O ye son of a whore.*

They walked on down the winding path of the garden toward a small gold-roofed pavilion, banners of radiant white cloth waving from the peak of its sloping roof. The shadows of the banners fluttered on the bright grass, as Raker pondered the flow of memories that had begun to rise in him. He saw Arabia like a magic lantern shining and he was kneeling with the men by the campfire, praising the Leader of the Caravan. *He has no son, no father, no brother. None stands before his face.* The camels settled for the night, their bridles jingling softly as they lowered themselves to the sand.

The pavilion had a terrace of jade, to which Raker and the Sage ascended. A brilliant monkey sported there, swinging on the delicate tree limbs overhanging the terrace. Raker sailed through memory toward a woman in gleaming tights. The French countryside was below, and her lips were red as she caught him and swung him, back to the trapeze tower. Her arms were strong, her presence on the high wire awesome, concentrated. In the night she was a lover, and in the last swooning, when they fell together into the crowd, when they struck the ground in death, then the fires of the circus seemed most bright, and he sensed the spirit of romance, fluttering in the air, in sequins, turning, escaping to the high clouds.

The pavilion had benches of wood. The Porcelain Sage, sitting cross-legged in his robes, smiled. "The contemplation of the ages," he said, turning over his hand, extending it palm upward toward the rosy sun of the Paradise, and he froze there in the posture, his face uplifted.

© © ©

MRS. BONDYJIG WAS BENT over bare-naked in the bomb shelter, her head against the gas pedal of the armored van. The Germans were attacking London from above, while Perky attempted Mrs. Bondyjig from behind, kneeling against her great rump, his arms extended around her waist so that his hands met her massive .50 millimeter boob-fruits, which he squeezed for high tea as the bomb shelter shuddered and creaked.

"Oh, Mr. Perky."

Flickering light from the main room of the bomb shelter came under the door of the van. The hermit was able to drive happily through the gears in this position, detouring past the lady's hind cheeks, which, though tremendous, could be bulldozed aside somewhat. His machine gun was temporarily out of ammunition, all fifty cases having been fired into the sky, and so he was amusing himself on this little traveled route, along scenic canals not mentioned in *Baedeker*.

Mrs. Bondyjig slowly rotated her behind, big as a barrel stove, so she could feel, to the right and left of her ham sandwich, Mr. Perky's length of bologna. It was positively Cro-Magnon, this club which had subdued her, and which hunted around now in the deep recesses of her bear's den. The paintings on the walls were of special interest to anthropologists from many countries, depicting as they did the hunt for the buffalo, the deer, and the larger birds, not to mention certain fertility symbols connected with springtime in England.

Perky threw himself into four-wheel drive, the only sure power for the dangerous holes on this dirt road. The mud oozed, made sucking noises, but his drive shaft continued its good job. If he had a pair of goggles and motoring gloves he might be taken for a Member of Parliament, driving out with the wife to meet constituents. A little of the family touch was sound politics. Lord Beaverboard had promised more ammunition, but of course there was a certain amount of red tape, particularly since the hermit had shot down a Royal Air Force supply plane, showering tins of bully beef over the neighborhood.

© © ©

SHE AND PROFESSOR MONTROSE walked along College Avenue, stopping outside a restaurant. Her apartment was above it. "Will you come up?"

He had to register next semester's students at the gymnasium; he stepped inside her doorway to say goodbye. She closed the door to the street. They were in a tiny vestibule with a staircase that led up to her apartment. Through the wall he could hear the noises of the restaurant.

"You have to go, don't you," she said, unzipping his fly.

"Yes, I'm late already."

She dropped slowly to her knees and kissed the

Professor's cock, taking it into her mouth as he gripped the railing of the stairwell. The sounds of the restaurant came clearer. A waitress was taking an order of cheesedogs. His knees were weakening. Her full lips passed back and forth in the half-light of the hallway.

"Must . . . sit . . . down," he said, sitting heavily on the stairs, as she blew him, her knees showing through her open trench coat.

A red flame burned her cheeks as she pressed them to it. "Am I your little cocksucker?" she asked deliriously, then returned to it furiously, until it erupted, exploding the warm drink back to her throat. She choked, swallowed, and drank more with her lips, smelling the secret life of him. I should like to bathe in it.

Montrose collapsed backward on the stairs. Orgasm 2, a full-credit course. Gentlemen, ladies, good afternoon.

She held it for a moment more, then put the descended member back into his pants, a beautiful skybird which must be allowed to return to its own realm. "You'd better go now," she said, raising herself on tiptoe; her shoes fell away from her heels as she kissed him on the mouth and he tasted himself.

"Yes," he said, picking up his briefcase. "Well, then . . ." Awkwardly, he put his hand to the door. He turned back to look at her. She was smiling, with deep female awareness in her eyes, satisfied, and planning seven more eternities of the same.

He walked along the street quickly, toward the gymnasium, where the spring semester enrollment was proceeding. He left the smell of the green lawns behind him and entered the stale perfume of athletes and their adorers. His feet echoed along the maze of corridors as he found his way into the huge main arena. The polished wooden floor was lined with desks and signs: One department after another was represented, with the specifics of their offering for the new term. He picked his way through the lines, until he reached his department. The Head of Philosophy, Professor Gaul, a large, grey-haired old nihilist with a loathing for metaphysical discussion, was supervising the activity. "Montrose," he said sternly, by way of greeting.

"Sir."

"We've told your students to come back when they see this table open." He pointed to where Montrose was to sit, before a large stack of IBM cards.

"Thank you, sir. I was delayed."

"Pandemonium, as usual." Professor Gaul surveyed the sea of bobbing heads, forming silently with his lips a characteristic vulgarity.

"How's it going, Al?" asked Professor Gash, at his desk to the left of Montrose. Montrose turned toward him, lightheaded, smiling.

"You've had some blocks removed," said Gash. "A man who's had some nookie has that certain look in his eye."

Montrose opened his table by turning around the small rectangular plastic block which bore his first initial and last name.

"Any levitating lamas lately, Montrose?" asked Associate Professor Wurt Cravis, at his own desk to the right of Montrose.

"Is this Eastern Philosophy?"

A demanding female voice brought Montrose out of his attempt to make sense of the IBM card system.

Blonde-haired, with the circular pin of some fraternity in the lapel of her pants suit, her blue eyes were as cold as the Arctic Ocean. She was going to run Eastern Philosophy through her machine, punching it neatly full of holes and filing it in the Void.

Sign here, here, and here. The hour, she suddenly realized, was in conflict with her Home Economics Course, coinciding with a two-hour stove seminar. Behind her a line of other students was forming, with the usual suspicious glances and stupefied stares.

Montrose felt the moment blossoming as time slowed down, and the blonde student, in an infinity of flickering film frames, formed a word on her lips. In the slowness of its coming, Montrose made completely certain that he knew what he was doing, examining his margin of sanity, which seemed healthy enough and, as time resumed its normal count, before the girl's word was full out, he was far gone, leaving the desk, the gymnasium, striding out into the day. The sky was wonderfully blue, as the continuing signal of the correctness of his move, and the grass smelled sweet as he descended, down into town, quickly through the alley, across the parking lot, into his cellar, where he packed his Eastern texts and his few clothes.

Later, after waiting only briefly in the bus terminal, so short a time that he became all the more certain he was traveling with the current, he embarked on a bus. The windows were shaded green. He looked at the old campus, feeling like a fish returned to its bowl after a brief flop on the floor. The bus went down College Avenue, toward the highway, passing the restaurant and her doorway. He looked at her windows as they flashed in the sunlight, and were gone, behind.

◎ ◎ ◎

DESPITE THE SUNLIGHT coming into Reverend Cupplewaite's sitting room, Sally Fifer's feet were cold. *Feet like that,* Mother said, *make a man jump out of bed.* "Have you ever seen a man riding one of those big logs down river?" asked Sally. She stirred her spoon in the tea, swirling the dark liquid.

"The French fellows are quite good at it, I understand," said Reverend Cupplewaite. He took a sip of tea, holding it for a moment in his mouth, then swallowing it. "I believe this table is French," he said, indicating the spindly-legged piece beside his chair. "Of course, I can't be certain. Most of the furniture was here when I moved in."

"They're all lovely things," said Sally.

"Yes," said Reverend Cupplewaite, "yes, they are." He ran his finger across the top of the presumably French table, stopping with his nail in the joint of each piece of wood. As a child he'd often dug at pieces of soft wood with his finger, or with a knife, though nothing shapely ever came of it. Still, the boring gave him a certain pleasure, and it was this pleasure he took now, running his carefully trimmed nail in the groove of the wood.

Sally Fifer brought her own hand to the table top, running her fingers on the polished wood, close to the Reverend's probing.

He looked for a moment, fascinated, at the slim white hand on the table, then picked up his teacup and lifted it to his lips. "This tea," he said, looking out the window, "comes all the way from India."

Sally repeated the name of that country, too far away even for her imagination, though she'd been in a teashop once, as a girl, along the waterfront of a seaport town, and she remembered the tea chests, stamped with exotic names. There had been a map on the wall behind the teaman's counter. It was this map she brought to her mind now, trying to remember if India were on it, but she could only revive a dull shape on faded paper, hanging on the bygone wall.

"The world," said Reverend Cupplewaite, holding the teacup up in his two hands, studying its rim. He felt the raw material of a sermon rising, but he let it go unheeded. "India," he repeated, bringing the cup to his lips and closing his eyes as the tea came to his tongue again.

© © ©

O THE TAY ROAD O

"Hello, Herman, how are ye?"

"Who's that. I caint see ye. I'm havin' . . . a fit."

"It's Willis Creek, ye crazy old son of a whore, ye remember me."

His arm come through mine. The dark awful cloud is blowin' away. I see him, an old feller, like me. There's his shack down the path.

"Come on in awhile, Herman," he says. "Put yer wagon down."

I set the old whore down and we walks down the path. Rivers come out o' his eyes, 'cause his name is Creek. Step inside his shack. Little place, whirlin', swirlin'. "Yer chair is floatin' in the air."

"Is it now? Well, goddamn ye . . ." He grab it, smack it down solid. "Sit on the son of a whore, Herman, and keep 'er quiet."

"Thanks." I sit on 'er. "How be ye?"

"Waitin' ter flop over." An old feller like me. Where the rivers come out o' his eyes, they's stone and sand.

"I ain't been right in the head." says I.

He pokes the stove with his iron. "It's the rare bird that is."

"I see plenty a strange thing," says I.

"It's plenty strange," says he. "I heerd things in the night."

"Did ye? Did ye now?"

"One night," says he, "a feller come in the cabin. He was from up country. Said his name was Pine. And he cut my Jesus head off. I sat right up in bed. I felt all around where me head should be."

"Gone?"

"Gone."

The fire jumps up in the stove, cracklin' on the dry wood. "I don't let 'er bother me none," he say, takin' a smoke out o' his pocket.

"But," says I, "the sky blows open. I see a dead man comin' acrosst the field, big, like this, a-walkin'." I git up and show him, movin' me arms.

"Caint hurt ye, Herman," says he. "Ain't nawthin' kin hurt ye. I knowed this since I come eighty."

"Ye ain't afeared n'more?"

"If Pine come in here this minute and say he want the rest o' me, ter chop up and feed ter the whiskey jacks, he kin, 'cause . . ." He's birds and trees now. He's a mountain speakin'. ". . . 'cause I ain't nawthin' ter begin with!" He light up his smoke, a-laughin' an a-chokin', spittin' in the fire. "Haarrrggghhh, harrggghh, p-tweeeee!" He slap his knee, jist a-rockin' an' a-laughin'. "Ain't nawthin' in the first place, Herman. That's the Jesus joke, see. No son of a whore kin git me. I'm empty as that goddamn cook pot!" He give the pot a kick an' it go rollin' acrosst the floor.

It's jist as he say. The feller's empty. I kin see right through the bugger. I kin see right through the shack, the trees, the sky. It's all there, boys, but she's empty!

"Ain't it a son of a whore of a thing," says he, smilin', rockin' easy in his chair.

© © ©

CORPORAL RAZAMOV FOLLOWED her up-stairs. The Lieutenant cheered at the foot of the stair-case, saying that Corporal Ghost would soon be re-born. He followed her down the hallway to a room. The Lieutenant's voice could be heard through the floor, threatening the landlord with death. The music of a violin came through the floor, and Razamov watched her dance, turning half-naked for him, in a peasant step, her breasts, her belly moving in shadows. He heard other women's voices joining the soldiers downstairs, as she turned, completely naked. He saw in the candlelight, in the yellow glow: Her mound was hairless.

"Well, Corporal, how do you feel now?" asked the Lieutenant.

Razamov sat in their carriage, staring out the window. "I gave her a jewel worth one hundred and fifty thousand rubles."

"She's worth it, old fellow, I quite agree."

They wandered by the river. The river birds circled, calling. The men slept on the bank all morning as the sun rose, and in the afternoon they called upon two sisters, close friends of the Lieutenant's.

"And what do you do, Corporal?"

"I guard a flower."

"How amusing!" Their salon overlooked the river. They sat at a marble-topped table, drinking dark coffee.

"We're going for a ride, old fellow," said the Lieutenant. "Join us at the inn for supper."

"Do you love me?" she asked. It was night. The lights were on the river.

At the inn, he found himself stared at by the other sister. Her hair was long, brown, she seemed childlike. In the alley of the inn, when he and the Lieutenant were getting a breath of air, they planned the exchange.

"Do you love me?" she asked.

He fled on the following dawn and wandered alone through the city. Standing idly on the steps leading down to the river, a sudden and distant joy signaled to him. It seemed almost to be his in this hour, and yet, when he tried to understand the feeling, it was gone beyond him, far up river. The river birds circled, calling and diving. One floated on the current, flapping its wings, trying to lift a sparkling object from the water.

Later, as he stood at the central square of the city,

where the holiday strollers talked and laughed, the feeling came again. He searched in himself for the clue to it. None of his memories was connected to it. Unlike the voice of the Devil, which he'd wrestled with in winter, its message seemed beyond madness.

He purchased pen and paper. The feeling was a poem of St. Petersburg.

chapter 10

THE LAVATORIES of the Golden Cafeteria are in the basement, at the bottom of a flight of narrow stairs. The walls are yellow, lit by two small bulbs at either end of the staircase. At the foot of the stairs is a small open area, given to a mop and pail. Beyond a heavy iron door is the boiler room. Next to it is a door marked *Gentlemen.* Through this door a Puerto Rican boy entered, making straight for the stalls, of which there were two, painted green.

One of the stalls, nearest the wall, was occupied, a pair of battered shoes and wrinkled trouser legs showing beneath the partition. The boy stepped into the unoccupied stall, closed the door, and lowered his pants. He did not sit on the toilet seat, but stood with his pants around his ankles, drawing with a Magic Marker a large erect penis on the stall wall, amidst other messages already scrawled there.

> I WILL BLOW YOU. LEAVE TIME
> AND PLACE.
> YOU GODDAMN FAGGOT
> WHAT DO YOU KNOW, HONEY?
> PLENTY YOU FAGGOT I'M A
> MARINE
> will some one please piss on me
> I'LL PISS ON YOUR GRAVE

After drawing the large erection on the wall, the boy signed his name, *Joséito,* on the shaft. He sat down, contemplating the drawn organ and his own. He looked toward the next stall, at the shoes and trousers. No sound or movement came from their owner. Joséito lit a cigarette, humming a song to himself. The trousers in the next stall moved. Joséito waited. A piece of toilet paper, neatly folded, was offered at the bottom edge of the partition separating the two stalls. Joséito took it and read: "May I help you?"

He slipped his small lithe body off the toilet seat and, facing the next stall, knelt, exposing his penis. He sang softly:

> *Qué bonita bandera*
> *Qué bonita bandera*
> *Qué bonita bandera*
> *Es la bandera Puertoriqueña*

waving his penis erotically in time to the song.

The organ was taken by lips, deftly, expertly. Joséito leaned his head against the stall wall. The lips performed quickly, wildly hungry. *O Mamacita, perfectamente!*

Rough hands gently caressed his testicles. Joséito sobbed with the tickling, then laughed loudly, waving his arms happily, accidentally breaking the face of his watch on the porcelain base of the toilet.

The lips took all, till he could stand it no longer. He withdrew his penis and quickly wiped it. He wanted to be gone and, pulling up his pants with great speed he fled the stall, not even stopping to comb his hair. He was up the yellow staircase swiftly, through the revolving door, and into the warm spring street. He hadn't done nothing. He was just walking along.

The man reading the *New York Times Book Review* in the window of the cafeteria did not look up when his companion returned from the lavatory.

"I just blew the most delicious child in the basement," said the grey-haired man, sitting back down at the table.

"Yes, Donald," said his friend, putting aside the *Book Review* and taking up the *Magazine* section.

© © ©

RAKER AND THE PORCELAIN SAGE walked the museum. It was quiet, except for the water-play of the ancient fountains. Through the corridors they went, slowly, examining the painting and sculpture, the golden headdresses. They stood before a vivid piece of India, the portrait of a musician, seated on a dais, performing with a stringed instrument. Music came from the painting, a winding serpentine theme which circulated in the gallery. The musician faded from the painting, and the colors which formed him regrouped into suns, moons, worlds, and the raga described the coming to birth and the passing of these worlds. Raker swelled with adoration of the cosmos as the showerfall of notes and the thumping of the drum overcame him.

The golden galaxy disintegrated and became a baby, playing with a beautiful rattle, which kept the rhythm of the music, and the baby grew older and studied music and became the musician on the dais, weaving the high song of love's magic dance.

"How grand, how grand!" said Raker, turning to the Porcelain Sage.

"Yes," said the Sage, "and the face of the player is so familiar."

The eyes and mouth and the angle of the jaw did seem familiar, but he could not remember where he'd seen the young man, so accomplished on his instrument and smiling now, his hair long and dark, his gown white, tied with a strand of fine rope.

"It is your next incarnation," said the Sage, taking Raker by the arm and leading him away, down the hall.

© © ©

LORD BEAVERBOARD RETURNED from African service with an eye patch, one of his orbs having been removed by the screen door of his jungle head-quarters in a shuffle-up with his batman. His Lordship struck a dashing figure in parliamentary procedure, and it was largely through his efforts that Douglas Perky was awarded a knighthood for his design of the original and most impregnable air-raid shelter of the war, in which the homeless had gathered, kept spirit, given birth.

The hermit ventured above ground to kneel before the Royal Family. His daylight walk was strange, somnambulistic, a primeval fish first flopping onto land. The bright light made him squint; his pale skin seemed luminous. Lord Beaverboard explained to the King that phosphorous deposits had been found in Sir Perky's hole, and his exposure to them made him glow, especially in the bright candlepower of the palace.

After the ceremonies of knighthood, Sir Perky returned to his underground chamber, now quiet and empty of urchins. Lord Beaverboard was with him. Lady Beaverboard and Mrs. Bondyjig were entertaining at the manor, and the festivities came to the two men like the faroff rumbling of a storm from which they'd found shelter. Sir Perky removed a bottle and two glasses from his liquor cabinet.

The two men downed the flaming shot, both their faces quivering for a moment. "Herr Hitler found bitter weeds in England," said Lord Beaverboard, adjusting his eye patch.

There was the sound of tumbling, then cursing, from the faroff entrance to the cavern. As footsteps resumed in the hallway, Sir Perky and Lord Beaverboard watched the door. A haggard, rumpled figure appeared through the shadows of the doorway.

"Honk of *The Times*. Fell down your bloody stairs."

" 'ave a drink," said Sir Perky, taking another glass from the cabinet and handing it to the dazed newspaperman.

"Much obliged. A bonk on the conk, possible concussion." He drained the glass without wincing and held it forth again. He looked at his hosts. "Lord Beaverboard and Sir Perky?"

"I am Lord Beaverboard. This is Sir Perky."

Newsman Honk drained off his second tumbler of whisky and set it down on the mosaic table in front of him, in which two geisha girls knelt, one playing a lute, the other serving tea. "Pleasant enough digs," he said. "Something like a mole, eh? What?" He tried to chuckle, then grabbed his forehead.

" 'ave another," said Sir Perky, refilling the newsman's glass.

"Sir Perky," said the newsman, taking out his notebook and pencil, "what are you going to do now that you're a knight?"

"Get some more ammo for the machine gun."

"Bit of target shooting, eh? Quite a bag, your having shot down the Prime Minister's secretary!"

"It was a small, unmarked plane," said Lord Beaverboard, defending the gunnery of his hermit. "In any case, the secretary was able to bail to safety. It was unfortunate, of course, that he landed in a tree inhabited by a rabid squirrel."

Sir Perky poured out tumblers of drink all around. London was in a festive mood. Mrs. Bondyjig was serving sandwiches. The Prime Minister's secretary was fully recovered, except for his strange propensity for hiding nuts in his desk drawer.

"People say you're something of a philosopher," said newsman Honk. "Principal influences?"

"I count the cracks in the ceilin'."

"You've read Bertrand Russell then?" Newsman Honk sipped his drink, placed the tumbler to his forehead.

"Can't read," said Perky.

"Not enough light down here, what?"

"Sir Perky is an original thinker," said Lord Beaverboard, draining his glass. Must get blotto. Rommel in the desert sands, creeping.

"Well, gentlemen, that should do it," said newsman Honk, closing his notebook. "I've got the bones of a good story here."

"We found some bones while we were blastin'," said Sir Perky. "The skull 'ad a ball in it."

"I daresay I've got one in mine," said the reporter and, standing, saluted Sir Perky and Lord Beaverboard with his glass, draining its contents with a final flip of the wrist. "You'll be hearing from my lawyer about the little tumble I took down your stairs, and in the meantime I'll file this story. Gentlemen, good day." He turned and went into the shadows of the hall.

◎ ◎ ◎

PROFESSOR MONTROSE WATCHED out the window as his bus wound down the great circle of highway that leads into the Lincoln Tunnel. Beneath the Hudson River, in the pale light of the tunnel passage, his excitement mounted. The Port Authority Building hummed with travelers; a huge clock turned in the center of the building. He stepped into the street, upon a great avenue, letting the cab driver recommend a small hotel on the Upper West Side, with a Chinese restaurant off its main lobby. The waiter treated him uncivilly, and the food was excellent.

He walked up winding Riverside Drive. Across the river, the lights of New Jersey came on, the glittering Palisades, the enormous Spry sign. Montrose stood at the Soldiers and Sailors monument, on a stone balustrade looking out on Riverside Park. On the dark paths below, he heard Spanish tongues, a girl, a boy.

He walked eastward, back to Broadway, past the flower stall to the tobacco shop, where he purchased a paper; a helicopter churned the night sky. Each doorway was a shop, a restaurant, a lighted place where the great city watched, drinking coffee, scheming, chasing women and dreams. In a pet shop, rows of fish tanks bubbled, in which sleeping silver forms were illuminated by pale night lights.

From the doorway of Bombay House came the smell of curry and the fanning sound of horns, the cry of a thousand birds answered by the strings of a sitar. Montrose stood in the doorway, listening to the scratchy record. The tables were lit by tiny lamps.

> *I am Time without end,*
> *The Sustainer,*
> *Everywhere.*

The supermarket was still open, bright, glaring. A black woman in sequined dress, like the skin of a fish, entered the luminous gloom of La Ronda bar, and Montrose walked on past.

◎ ◎ ◎

"THERE'S A CHILD in the village," said Sally Fifer, "doesn't feel a thing when she gets burned. But take that child in the snow, or get her feet cold, and doesn't she scream for an hour."

"Most peculiar," said Reverend Cupplewaite, folding his hands over his stomach, in which two pieces of Sally's cake floated, in tea.

"Well, you know, Jack the trapper once told my father that if he had a dream about an animal in the woods, he'd go to that spot in the woods next day, and the animal would be there." Sally set her cup down, almost defiantly, as if challenging the authority of the church, as invested in Reverend Cupplewaite.

"Indeed?" Reverend Cupplewaite was hungry for another piece of cake. Could he take another in front of the girl and still uphold the dignity of his office?

"Some folks say there's something . . . *demonic* . . ." Sally uttered the word fearfully, like a child trying to frighten herself. Reverend Cupplewaite took opportunity of her dramatic pause to slice himself off another wedge of cake. The office of the church, after all, is beyond pastry.

". . . demonic . . ." continued Sally, "on the Tay Road."

Reverend Cupplewaite arranged the cake in the center of his plate, as if another hand had placed it there, somewhat inefficiently, when he wasn't looking. He toyed with the questionable offering.

"Look," said Sally, getting up to the window, "there's Mr. Jorgen."

Cupplewaite looked past the white cloth of her dress, through the window to the road, where the old man was pulling his wagon, muttering to himself. The Reverend was uneasy with the fellow, who had once told him Jesus Christ's body was green and hung in the Tay forest. "His mind . . ." said Reverend Cupplewaite.

"Yes," said Sally, watching the wagon creak slowly past.

"Well," said the Reverend, "we've been having a spell of good weather lately."

"Haven't we!" said Sally, closing her eyes to the bright afternoon sun and seeing in her closed eyelids the silhouette, bright red, of the old man's wagon, like a chariot of fire.

◐ ◐ ◐

O THE TAY ROAD O the Jesus whoreson Tay Road, boys. Ropes tied around me, tied in knots I am, but she's an empty pot, boys, like the old feller say. Goddamn divils made it, cooked 'er up, quite a stew, Momma, she made me, but I couldn't eat no little rabbit.

Ain't that Reverend Copperhead's place, boys? Jesus cross in the garden, boys, that's the place. Hammered the poor feller up there. Ye put a nail in the horse's shoe wrong, he'll kick ye into Jerusalum. French feller come here oncet to shoe the odd horse, missed with the nail and drove 'er clear up into the quick of his hoof. Boys, that horse give it to 'im. Black horse in a white field means death. If a woodpucker taps on the side o' yer house, yer gonna move.

What did the feller do, boys, that he got hisself tacked on the whiffle tree?

Me hands, looky. Got holes there, clear through. Say, I remember why. Wouldn't eat no supper o' rabbits, and Momma said, you eat.

Won't eat no Jesus rabbit.

Well, I'll fix you, Mister, says Poppa. An' they nailed me on the tree. Sky is fierce with fire. Ground is shakin'. Black horse in a white field, won't let none come near 'im, 'cause he's got the nail in, up ta the quick.

Say, I'm hangin' here still, on the tree. Come and visit me. I hang here ferever. She's Jesus lonely on the tree, boys, every time.

◎ ◎ ◎

LIEUTENANT RAZAMOV was visited at his flower post by the Countess, who brought a small boy she said was his son, and they walked in the field, the child delighting in butterflies.

He showed the Countess his poetry. She kissed him sweetly and asked him if any of them were about her.

Empress Catherine, learning of Razamov's poems, had them sent for. Razamov was elated, certain the poems would be published, translated perhaps to the French, reaching the eyes of Voltaire and all Europe. Catherine, an avid reader, especially of history and political theory, gave the poems a careful reading. Not understanding them, she turned them over to her Intelligence Staff for decoding, for some cipher might be at work in the strange words.

Razamov was cleared. A Turkish collaborator he was not, nor a key figure in a *coup d'état*. Catherine, still uneasy, thinking that she was compromised somehow in the work, by the fact that her name was not mentioned, had them burned. With an elaborate letter of apology and the story of a fire (wooden palaces are so inflammable), she included a jewel, worth, she said, 200,000 rubles, which she hoped would in some way repay the loss, "my dear *Captain* Razamov."

chapter 11

THE LADIES' ROOM of the Golden Cafeteria has no art work on the stalls, no messages. It is a plain room, dull yellow. There is a sink, a mirror, a paper towel dispenser with no towels. Beside it is a sanitary napkin dispenser, used occasionally by employees only, for the majority of the Golden Cafeteria women are beyond such needs. One of them is standing a few feet from the sink. She is bent over at the waist. It is her permanent posture, she cannot straighten. She is feeling poorly. It comes and goes, and when it comes she must be alone, away from talk and the smell of food, and so she goes below to the Ladies', to stand bent over, near the mirror, never looking at it.

She clings to her life, has been clinging frantically for years, though often it seems on the verge of going, without her consent. She knows only those thoughts which analyze her ailment, its progress, its retreat, its holding. She feels it in her throat, a dark fountain which sometimes bubbles with secret, malignant gases. She knows it in her legs, which have swollen like cooked sausages. Her heart skips a beat, stopping completely for a moment, leaving her suspended. Will she return? She does, with renewed beat, though she must go to the cellar of the Golden and stand in the cool gloom, bent over by the sink, staring at the tiled floor.

There she regains her slim measure of confidence, certain she will live out the day. She climbs the stairs, then, one slow step at a time, wheezing as she goes. She does not wish to die in the cellar or on the stairs, but, if possible, in her hotel room, during sleep. She has lived out her death innumerable times, each time, at the end, railing against the trick life has played her, the widow of Mr. Eli Fink: she should be exempted. What are the scientists doing about it? There's a country—she read about it in the *Times*—where people live to be 200. Eli, Eli, give me a signal, a sign.

After a half-hour's climb, she reaches the top of the stairs. Bent, she emerges into the rattle of trays, into the bouquet of food, into life. She has been to the lair of the dragon and returned, clutching the precious pearl. The colorful desserts—pies of bright filling, Jell-O with whipped cream, sugar-dusted buns—fill her with hope. She remembers the good old days in the apartment at the Majestic Hotel, playing a game of cards with Mr. Fink and Mr. and Mrs. Klein, all together, nice. She turns toward her table, the regular place, three or four down from the window. Mrs. Naggy is there, talking with Mr. Bark, whose larynx has been removed. He speaks from some other part of the neck, deeper down, in rasping, muffled shouts. She hears him all the way across the cafeteria.

"HI GOG SUN BUDDER, MIZZ NAG."

She walks slowly toward them. Mr. Bark is buttering his bread. "GOG NIGHT DAY, HEY?"

She sits wearily in their midst, cannot lift her eyes just yet.

"How're you feeling," asks Mrs. Naggy.

"Don't ask."

"HI, MIZZ FIG!" Mr. Bark waves his butter knife. Mrs. Fink lifts the right corner of her mouth in twisted coquette smile. The left corner is paralyzed from a stroke.

◎ ◎ ◎

RAKER AND THE PORCELAIN SAGE climbed the stairs of the museum to the Hall of the Vases. Upon their exterior the pantheon of figures moved—mandarins in gold robes, ladies of high station, insects of spindly beauty and birds of love on flowering branches.

A simple white vase stood alone on its own shelf. The base was ovular, the neck a long slender stem. Its dignity was unadorned by scenery or figures. The Porcelain Sage bowed to the vase and froze in the posture of obeisance.

The vase glowed now with mysterious brilliance, brighter than the sun. Raker stood transfixed in its

clear light, which covered him, filled the hall, the entire museum. Swooning, he entered the brilliance, recalling again the hour of his death and the ages of
tranquillity he'd spent in the light. He had this dream:
He was in a Manhattan penthouse at a cocktail party.
The hostess looked at him, began to smile, when a sudden veil of anxiety crossed her face. Raker turned to
the window. A brilliant light appeared outside, then
flashed into the room, turning everyone in the room
and all its contents white, as the sound of a thousand
thunders reverberated in the city.

"The fools," sobbed Raker, "the blind, bitter fools
who have dropped it" and, shielding his wife from the
fireflash of the bomb, he prepared to die.

Out of the thousand thunders came the overwhelming sound of birds. Raker felt the flutter of their
wings all around his head. They landed upon him,
cooing. He looked to the window. It was filled with
singing white doves, and they filled the room, soft and
musical.

                                                             © © ©

"THOSE WOULD BE THE BONES of Sir Rogerfurr Beaverboard, the first lord of the manor," said
Lord Beaverboard, staring into his whisky cup, feeling
the swirl of his ancestry.

Sir Perky opened a small French memento cabinet of wood and glass, taking out the clean, yellowed
skull of Sir Rogerfurr and setting it down on the table,
atop the subtly smiling geishas.

At the sight of the ancestral skull, Lord Beaver-

board felt the expanse of his family in the twickering
flylight of the chamber's lamp. "A ball of lead between
the brows," he said and, like Aristotle contemplating
the bust of Homer, he gazed upon his romantic ances-
tor. "I say, Sir Perky, I believe I'm having an epiph-
any."

"The bathroom is out of the door and to yer right,
Lord B."

"O Sir ancient Rogerfurr," intoned the drunken
Lord, addressing the venerable skull.

The voice of Lord Beaverboard echoed in the
rooms of the catacomb, waking the numerous dead
from their sleep. His head felt like stone and bone. In
black cloaks and hoods, the encrusted dead appeared.
He touched the dark cloth of their cloaks, feeling the
stone bodies beneath, and a shiver passed through
him, like a fish twitching on a line.

"Takin' a chill, Lord Beaver?" Sir Perky poured
another glass of whisky for the Lord.

"Our illustrious family," said Lord Beaverboard,
raising his glass, clicking it against Sir Perky's. "Sir
Perky, I address you from the land of the dead. I have
made contact with my ancestry." He stroked the skull
of his forebear.

"I like to look at the earth walls," said Sir Perky,
"with their little roots stickin' out."

"They live down a stone staircase," said Lord
Beaverboard, pouring himself another drink and peering into the black eyeholes of the skull. "There are
some wooden rooms, the hardest of woods, stained very
dark."

"Sounds like a pretty good place," said Sir Perky.

"I am happy to report there are smoking rooms,"

said Lord Beaverboard, "for gentlemen only. Unfortunately, there are great numbers of priests in them."

"The clergy likes a good cigar," said Sir Perky.

"Give Sir Rogerfurr a drink, old man," said Lord Beaverboard.

Sir Perky went to the cabinet, fetching another whisky tumbler, which he filled.

"Very good," said Lord Beaverboard. "Sir Rogerfurr will assimilate the bouquet if we leave it here before him." The tumbler was set in front of the smiling skull, whose forehead was shattered.

"Who put the ball in 'is noggin?" Sir Perky lit a cigar and placed it in the teeth of the skull, where it burned slowly, as if in an ash tray.

"It was, so they say, a hunting accident."

"Right between the eyes."

"It does seem rather peculiarly placed, doesn't it?" Lord Beaverboard fingered the death-ball. "Perhaps . . . ," he sighed, touching his eye patch, ". . . a careless servant."

"Or some little biscuit."

"The passions of Monday," said Lord Beaverboard, opening his collar, for his brain was flushed, "turn to stone on Tuesday."

"Yoohoo, Sir Perky!" The voice of Mrs. Bondyjig echoed through the still cavern, shattering the ancestral procession. The dead fled into their hidden niches. Lord Beaverboard sat stupefied. Sir Perky stood to welcome Mrs. Bondyjig and, behind her, Lady Beaverboard.

"Lord Beaverboard," said Lady Beaverboard, "you simply must come up now. Winston will be arriving at any moment. What is that horrible smoking bone?"

"Sir Rogerfurr Beaverboard, my beloved sire," said Lord Beaverboard, standing and bowing toward the skull.

Lord Beaverboard was led quietly from the room by his wife. Mrs. Bondyjig looked coyly at Sir Perky. "What have you two old sots been up to?" She had lost fifteen pounds, and felt girlish from champagne.

"Come here," said Sir Perky, "and feel my 'orrible smokin' bone."

"Please, Sir Perky!"

◑ ◑ ◑

MEN WANTED

In his hotel room in the morning, ex-Professor of Philosophy Montrose circled the ad for the Warren Street Employment Offices. He dressed in suit and tie, carried the newspaper under his arm, received instructions in the subway, and rode the grim underground car to Warren Street at the foot of the island.

He climbed the subway stairs into the bright morning and walked along Warren Street toward the Hudson River. Many men stood in front of the huge employment building. Inside was a greater crowd of men—blacks, Latins, Europeans—in working caps and jackets, wrinkled suits, in various states of drunkenness, laughing in the halls, smoking, talking, mumbling to themselves as they read the lists of jobs which were written on pieces of cardboard and tacked up over the different doorways.

Each door opened into an employment office. Montrose walked up and down the hall, scanning the jobs, sharing his job-hunting urge with a desire to flee this block of flesh-peddlers. He stepped inside a doorway, into a room filled with folding chairs on which men sat talking, sleeping, reading old newspapers. A rough voice called out from beyond the counter at the front of the room: "I need a dishwasher for the afternoon. Brooklyn."

A black man seated alongside Montrose said to himself, "Fuck that, man."

A tired old white man, pants bagged at the knees, suit jacket drooping off his shoulders, stood and walked slowly to the railing which separated the owner of the Ace Placement Office from the job applicants. "You know how to wash dishes?"

"I wash dish," said the old man, making a feeble gesture with his right hand.

"Gimme a buck and get goin'," said the owner, handing him a slip of paper. "Here's the address."

The old man fished a crumpled dollar bill from his pocket, put on his battered hat and shuffled out the door.

"I help you, mac?" The owner called to Montrose, who was still standing by the doorway in his University Shop tweeds.

"Yes," said Montrose, walking forward.

"Fill out an application," said the owner, thrusting a pink card and a pencil into Montrose's hand.

In the space marked *Education*, Montrose wrote *Ph.D. Philosophy Pennsylvania State University.* Beside *Job Preference*, he wrote *dishwasher* and returned the card.

The owner of the placement office called Montrose to a chair beside his desk and looked at the application card. He chewed on a dead cigar. "Ph.D. Philosophy. You kiddin' me?"

"Unfortunately, no."

The owner looked at Montrose as if at a piece of meat which might be a bargain if it wasn't rotten. He sniffed suspiciously and opened the drawer of his desk, taking out a paper cup the size of a shot glass and a plain brown medicine bottle. He poured a light brown liquid into the paper cup and drank it down, smacking his lips with a small gasp.

"If you're on the level, I could use you here." He pointed to an empty desk, on which a telephone was ringing. He answered it from his own extension, giving Montrose time to think. *You are privileged by higher education. You saw the kind of man who washes dishes.*

The placement manager hung up the phone, looked at Montrose. "I can see you're a professional man. You had to get away from the University, right? What was it, divorce?"

"Yes."

"I have a good eye for people. People." The placement manager smiled, warming to himself. "They're my business." He pointed across his desk to the collection of stragglers that sat in his office, waiting for the call. "I need an assistant. I'll start you at a hundred bucks a week. You'll get to meet all kinds of people, teach you plenty of philosophy. You can start right now. There's your desk and a file of applicants. When the phone rings and they want somebody, you've got 'em, in that file."

"I want to be a dishwasher."

The placement manager looked immediately into his job book, scribbled off an address, and handed it to Montrose. "Nedicks needs a counterman. Gimme fifteen bucks."

"You gave the old man a dishwashing job for a dollar."

"That was for one day, yo-yo. This is full time. Now if you'll excuse me, I've got another gentleman waiting." The placement manager opened his desk and poured another dose of medicine into his paper shot glass.

Montrose walked the hallway, through the ranks of men, feeling the weight of their oppression, their indifferent seeking, the complaints of their wives and consciences, their self-hatred, their thirst. In the lobby, in the sunlight coming through the glass doors, three black men were harmonizing a song.

It was nearing eleven o'clock, and the New York sun was already hot. He slung his suit jacket over his shoulder and rode the subway uptown toward the other end of the island. At the head office of Nedicks, he encountered another placement officer. She handed him an application. Under *Education* he wrote *high school.*

"Did you graduate?" she asked, handing him another sheet of paper.

"Yes," said Montrose, looking at the paper. It was a mathematics test.

"Write in your answers and hand it back to me," said the girl.

Montrose stood at the counter which separated them and worked out the mathematics problems. He worked them once, twice, three times, making sure, then handed her the paper. He watched, horrified, as she corrected it. He had two wrong answers.

"Are you sure you graduated?" she asked, looking down at him. She seemed to be seated on a towering pillar.

"No," he said, straining his neck backward to see her, "I didn't graduate."

"I didn't think so," said the girl. "You should never lie on an application. It goes against you. In view of that and your poor score on the test . . ." She looked at him, smiling indifferently. "A counterman has to be able to do math. I'm sorry. We'll keep your application on file."

Montrose stepped into the one o'clock sun. He was hungry. He went to a nearby Nedicks and had a grilled cheese sandwich.

"What happened?" The owner of Ace Placement opened the gate to his desk, and Montrose walked in.

"I flunked the entrance exam."

"Why you wanna get in that racket anyway?"

Montrose was hot, tired, confused. The four floors of the Warren Street Employment Offices were quiet. Afternoon was not job time. "I just want to wash dishes," he said.

"You want to wash dishes." The owner went through his book. "He wants to wash dishes." He pulled out a yellow card. "Report tomorrow morning at seven o'clock. I'll call now and tell them to expect you."

"Thanks," said Montrose, standing up.

"You won't have to wear a tie."

Montrose walked away, toward the door of the office. The black man he'd seen there in the morning was still there, asleep in his chair, waiting for the call.

© © ©

REVEREND CUPPLEWAITE WENT FURTHER into his chocolate cake, breaking off a piece that had the firm bottom and the gooey top as well. The southern sky through his window was still beautifully bright. The Reverend felt delicious in the region of his navel, a light tickle spreading outward, pulsating, like the sun. "This is extraordinary cake."

"I put several eggs into the icing," said Sally Fifer, blushing.

"Very healthful."

"Sarah Berry's mother isn't too good," said Sally.

Reverend Cupplewaite felt himself being drawn down, darkened, bliss destroyed. He would have to sit with another sick old woman, finding himself, as usual, with nothing to say, staring at withered hands, hearing faint, desperate breathing, and the final belch of the spirit as it fled his presence.

"She had the fever and was raving," said Sally.

"Most unfortunate." He'd seen fever-ridden old women before, and it upset him. "I suppose your father has his winter wood cut already?"

"Oh, yes," said Sally, smiling at the thought of her father's large muscled frame bringing down the gleaming ax in the dooryard. "Though he says there are some in this valley will go cold because they're too lazy to chop a few sticks of wood."

"I daresay."

"The dear knows Father's not one to put off such a thing."

"Have you seen any deer?"

"Father shot one last week. We'd just finished dinner when he stood up and said, 'In the north pasture, there's a deer feeding by the moon.' He killed it alright, just like he said, in the north pasture. How do you suppose he knew it was there?"

"Remarkable," said Reverend Cupplewaite.

"Well, don't we have venison every night."

"Delicious, venison." Reverend Cupplewaite was in no mood for dinner. Still he could appreciate it.

"The head is out by the barn if you want to see it," said Sally.

Reverend Cupplewaite did not want to see a fly-covered head out by the barn. He wanted to see Vienna. There was a travel book in the library of the church house, with a picture captioned, *"Ah, Vienna, city of my dreams!"* Perhaps there would be a world religious council; he saw himself walking with high-up religious leaders of Europe, who were listening keenly to his discourse on the life of the simple country preacher, of intimate contact with the flock. They would stand by the great rose-marble fountain in the travel-book, in their black habits, the sun of Vienna reflected brilliantly off the water.

"Jeffrey Block has a huge canker sore on his lip again," said Sally.

© © ©

O THE TAY ROAD O

Sometimes it's oats. Sometimes it's bran. Horse gits worms ye give 'im ashes an' bread. The worms goes fer the bread an' gits the ashes. Ashes is poison ter a worm. I seen worms long as snakes on the stable floor. On the Tay Road, boys, she's a long worm a-windin' round hersel'.

Hello dark man, say the horseflies.

"Hello, hello." Got a thousand eyes. See like me,

a thousand things. The day, the day. I'm a-burnin'.
I'm a-flyin', away, boys, inter the sun. I ain't comin'
back n'more. This is me last Jesus time on the Tay
Road O.

WHEN EMPRESS CATHERINE TURNED sixty,
she was seized again by the desire to visit the flower.
She came in pomp, with gold coach, honor guard,
maidens, and her lover, Prince Potemkin of Taurida,
who sniffed the air like a great horse. Throughout the
visit, he seemed distracted, listened to no one, could
only stare at the flower, for he, unlike Catherine, was a
mystic and sensed the extraordinary daemon that
haunted the field and had incarnated in the flower,
ruling, through it, an Empress.

The ladies-in-waiting played in the field. The soldiers stood watching, flirting. Potemkin went down on
one knee before the blossom, aware that empires were
crude artifice, compared to certain more subtle de-
signs, heaven-ruled. Within the white corolla he sensed
a wise and immaculate ruler. He could see the shim-
mering court she ruled and he felt the presence of le-
gions, more vast than the Russias, and cursed himself
again for having succumbed to Catherine's entreaties
that he leave his monastic life for her palace. She
threw him jewels and title, placed her court in his
hand, and he exchanged his lonely meditations for
power. But across his power there was a shadow. Yes,
he sensed a snare; perhaps he was already in the trap.

Catherine and Razamov sat in the tent. The Star

of the North had grown heavier, no longer wore her regimental uniform, preferring to hide her figure in a long gown. "So this has been your life," she said, still fascinated by the simplicity of his quarters, the same wooden desk, same bunk. "Do you remember . . . ?" She touched his hand.

Captain Razamov and Prince Potemkin stood together as Catherine stepped into the magnificently gilded coach.

"They say you've been here twenty-five years." Potemkin pointed his jewel-encrusted sword to the field.

"Twenty-six," said Razamov.

"What do you make of it?" Potemkin stepped into the coach, remaining in the ornate doorway.

Razamov stood silent. Potemkin hesitated, as if wanting to say more, then slipped into the silk cushions beside the aging autocrat.

"Well, Golden Pheasant," she said, "did you enjoy my flower?"

Two years later Potemkin was dead, killed in Catherine's campaign against the Turks. Captain Razamov's son fought in the same campaign and returned to visit his father. Razamov presented the lad with the second of Catherine's jewels. His son was twenty-four and made good use of the money—in horses, pistols, and women.

1
2
3
4
5
6
7
8
9
10
11

chapter 12

THE DISHWASHER HAD BEEN ON THE WAGON for nine months. Now that was done, and he was drunk, goddamnit, good and goddamn drunk, drunk and going to stay drunk.

He staggered along Broadway in the night, stopping in every one of the bars he had so carefully avoided for nine months. He'd walked by them every day, trying to block out the sound of drinking voices, holding his breath so he wouldn't smell stale beer blowing through the door.

Yesterday he lingered in the wave of voices and was glad they didn't have such a hold on him anymore. And he stood for a second in the smells, turning

171

to the diamond-shaped window in the door and he saw an old whore smiling, like the old days, and he went, Jesus Christ almighty give me a drink quick.

Whiskey, whiskey, whiskey. Three o'clock in the morning whiskey and I got plenty money for more whiskey, makes a man feel frisky, give me just one more whiskey.

He had drunk all night and slept on a bench and reported to work by force of habit, reeling through the kitchen, and he sang a little song for the Chinese cookie, by God, a little drinking song of old Broadway. And went right to his work. But he couldn't hold it like he used to, nosir! When you're not used to it, whiskey can backfire on you, good old whiskey can, and he puked quite suddenly in the dishwashing machine.

"Gimme another two fingers of Johnny Walker Red," he said to the barman, "and a glass of cold beer." And let's drink to the old days. I'm getting old. And he remembered New York when there were horse-drawn buggies in the streets and plenty of big ships in the harbor.

© © ©

THE METROPOLITAN MUSEUM underwent extensive renovation in 1969–70. For a while there was a great deal of dust over everything. The hallowed places of certain statues and paintings were changed, though the Chinese vases held their familiar spot, on the second floor, on either side of the huge staircase. Illuminated fountains were added to the museum entrance way. The Great Hall gained several gardens of rubber plants and flowers, framed with wooden benches.

St. John of the Cross, carved from wood, his eyes painted, continues to stare down the Spanish Hall.

Venus lays on her couch, with a wisp of cloth across her thighs, played to by a boy on a lute. Through the painted window behind her can be seen the green fields of an old day.

The body of Julius Raker is quietly removed, through the subterranean passageways of the museum, past those treasures which are stored below, awaiting their time and space above.

© © ©

THE ORNAMENTAL HERMIT, though old, was still in his hole. The Beaverboard estate had been sold to pay the tremendous settlement brought in favor of newsman Honk, who demonstrated once again the true power of the press in his most damaging series of articles about Lord Beaverboard's political career, which series prejudiced the courts in favor of the "concussion settlement," as it was called, which wiped Lord Beaverboard out and allowed newsman Honk to retire from journalism into a life of leisure. He tried to purchase the Beaverboard estate, but was beaten at this by a documentary film-maker, whose wife did not approve of the hermit remaining in the grounds.

"It's not his food," said the wife, "it's his electric bill."

"I can't make the old fellow live in an unlit tunnel, can I?" said her husband, staring over his grapefruit, through the dining room window, to the early-morning lawns.

"An old folks home is the place for him. He'd have plenty of nice friends his own age."

"The man's a hermit, darling. Can't stand people."

"You seem to get along with him."

"I'm going to make a film of the old boy: '*Looking Backwards* looks at London, the Blitz, the bomb shelter and the man—Sir Douglas Perky.' "

The great klieg lights were lowered into Sir Perky's hole. Miles of wire wound through his tunnels. The cameras turned, following Sir Perky through the passages, "which once sheltered England's homeless besieged, isn't that correct, Sir Perky?" The interviewer and Sir Perky stood in the central room, the circular hub of the wheeling labyrinth.

"Old Bondyjig and I spent the war in that machine," said Sir Perky, pointing with his cane to the sunken armored van. The crews instinctively shielded their lenses. The old coot was liable to strike with his stick at anything.

"Bondyjig? That would be . . ." The interviewer was a young man, and not all the Great Names of the War were familiar to him.

"Mrs. Bondy." Sir Perky's eyes were gleaming in the klieg lights, but squinted, like a rat caught in a flash. He walked over to the armored van, empty now, dusty. "Dead," he said, pointing with his cane to the shadowy interior.

"Yes, well," said the interviewer, "isn't it true that Churchill paid you a visit here?"

"Different fellers dropped in."

"Looking back, Sir Perky, what stands out most in your mind about that time of heroic struggle?"

"Time? It's a quarter past four."

"The war, I mean."

"One night I counted every crack in the main ceilin'. It wasn't easy because we 'ad a lot of little buggers runnin' around 'ere at the time."

"This is Lyle Fleetbath, *Looking Backwards*, with Sir Douglas Perky, in his original bomb shelter. Good . . ."

"There was more than a million of them."

". . . night."

"Cracks, I mean, not buggers."

The music ascended, filling the tunnel with the *Looking Backwards* theme. As planned, hermit Sir Perky climbed into his armored van and up to his machine gun turret, which had been loaded with a chain of live ammunition which the hermit would fire, giving a dynamic touch to the finale of the program. The director cued in the cameras that were covering the action above ground.

The hermit opened fire on an American advertising dirigible which was passing over at that historic hour, puncturing its gas bag and bringing it to earth in a spectacular flame-out caught in the color cameras of *Looking Backwards*. The show was cited for special mention in the House of Lords and won the London Drama Critics Award, Sir Perky receiving the bronze Swan of Avon statuette. His hole was declared a national monument.

◎ ◎ ◎

MONTROSE WALKED UP Broadway in the morning. At six-thirty, it is a quiet street. An occasional night man is mopping out a barroom doorway; a drunk weaves along, singing an old Broadway song. Montrose looked again at the slip of paper with the address of his new job. He looked at the number of the revolving door in front of him. He was there.

The door was locked. Montrose peered in the huge picture window, could see movement in the far back, in the kitchen. He circled the block, going to the back door of the cafeteria. The night man showed him where to put his jacket, gave him an apron. "You the dishwasher," he smiled.

The cooks were at their stoves, stirring cereal, cracking eggs. At seven o'clock the Golden Cafeteria opened, and shortly afterward Montrose was at the dishwashing machine, piling in the dirty dishes, stacking up the clean.

By the time the lunch hour was over, he was soaking wet, from water and sweat. On his own lunch break he went to the long table in the kitchen, carrying a plate of vegetables and cheese with bread. He was joined by a few of the other men, while a skeleton staff kept slinging food.

Wooden counters, metal pots, iron pans, black stove, white aprons, the voices, the smells . . . Montrose watched the head cook, a Chinese, whose arms were long, stretched from holding heavy cook pots. The arms remained close to his body, for some parts of the cooking area were narrow, and his arms had found their own best posture, close in, and the muscles had settled that way.

Montrose finished his meal and relaxed, only vaguely aware of himself. Mostly, he was the kitchen, the great service, and while washing dishes he was completely gone in the flood of water and the flow of the conveyor belt.

Then he picked himself up and returned to the dishes, sending without deliberation his hands into the scalding water. He felt no pain. He was deep into the pots and pans, scrubbing, making their surfaces shine happily. New York, a kitchen, the world: Montrose held the treasure. It was a heavy dish, of white, with a thin circular line painted around its inner plane.

◎   ◎   ◎

REVEREND CUPPLEWAITE put his feet up onto the soft misshapen hassock just beyond his chair. His black ecclesiastical shoes rocked back and forth as he tapped the toes together. This kind of day was his favorite, a sitting back and relaxing day. The leather chair gave off its customary smell—vaguely animal, partly human, soft, warm, an old friend, the repository of impressions left by a line of clergymen. He took another small piece of cake. "We've not had any rain for some days," he said, popping the morsel into his mouth.

"When we get a red sunset, that's the time," said Sally.

"I prefer the dry weather," said the Reverend. "Keeps the joints from acting up."

"Don't my knuckles smart in the wet," said Sally. "But you ought to drink some Labrador tea."

"Eh?"

"You can pick it in the fields around here. It's an old Indian remedy. You seep the leaves all day. Ed Smiles had the stiffness so bad he couldn't walk, until he drank Labrador. He's spry enough now, I imagine." He'd once asked her to dance, at the church social, but she'd refused, for the Reverend had been there.

"I must try that sometime," said Reverend Cupplewaite.

"I'll brew some for you," said Sally, happy in the direct promise of another meeting.

Reverend Cupplewaite liked to be ministered to, nothing so serious as marriage, of course, but all the flutterings just this side of it he considered to be rightfully his through the natural channels of his office, women's pies and so forth, small offerings, surely.

"The old remedies are best," said Sally.

Could he, dare he, take another piece of cake? It would be his third, fourth? Did it matter, in any case, to Sally? And finally, what did Sally matter? A man must be free. "I understand the spring thaw swept a bridge away down at Mackaquack," he said, and deftly, as if to illustrate the torrent that tore the bridge from its foundations, he sliced and slipped another piece of cake to his plate.

"They say the water was up around the treetops there," said Sally.

"Remarkable."

"Some cows got drowned." Sally saw them, bossies floating, bloated, upside down.

"Most unfortunate, indeed." Reverend Cupplewaite advanced on the new cake, to quickly shape it
like the old, not wanting it to appear so fresh to his
plate. We are weak, Lord, and You are strong. And he
poured himself a bit more tea.

◎ ◎ ◎

O THE TAY ROAD O

Feller up ahead, got his cart stuck in the ditch
look like. A person could git stuck a million year. I
been stuck here longer.

"Howdy," says I.

Thin feller, sittin' on his buckboard. Horse standin' by, sweatin'. "Son of a whore's played out," he
say, spittin' on the ground.

I know this feller from somewheres. He been stuck
here a million year too. "Well, let's give 'er a push,"
says I, a-goin' ter the back wheel.

"Gidd-up there, you!" he shout, and we three
give 'er all we got. Mud make suckin' noises. Wheels
buried ter the axletrees. She's stuck, boys.

"Son of a whore."

"Be here another million year."

"Aye."

The dust starts a-flyin' up the road. Here come a
fierce black nag, a-steppin', an' a young feller ridin'
her back. "Who's this feller?" says I.

"It's Tom Hawkey, likely."

Here's the young feller, with suns poppin' out o'
him, all over. "Trouble?"

"Stuck."

"By the Lord Jesus," says he, "we'll get 'er out o' there." His suns are blazin'. You kin hardly look at the young feller, he's sa bright. We hitch his black nag onter the wagon, next ta the other nag.

"There, by the snappin'-eyed Jesus," says the young feller, an' he gits in front o' his black horse, holdin' her bridle. He's one sun now, a-blazin'. His nag is the black night wi' stars. We all git behind the wheels. "Gee-yup, goddamn ye!"

The wagon she lifts up an' out, onter the road.

"Holy-o-Jesus, she didn't take much o' that, did she?" The young feller lit up fer miles.

© © ©

CATHERINE DIED in the lavatory, of a stroke. The 19th century venerated her as the builder of a great power, rival to all Europe. The flower guard was kept in her memory by a succession of soldiers, first under the direct command of Captain Razamov, and after his death through the official channels of his regiment. At the time of the revolution in 1917, an old man, the last of the guards, was still watching the flower, but threw over his post to storm the palace with the peasants.

Historians maintain that a poet named Razamov did exist during the time of Catherine, was something of a madman, never saw military service, and dreamt the entire account of the flower, which popular imagination wove into the final form of the legend, including the succeeding Guards of the Flower, whose last member, nonexistent, stormed the gates of Nicholas II.